CT FAVXBOVRGS DE PARIS AVEC LA DESCRIPTION DE SON *ANTIQVITE* *& SINGVLARITEZ*

Charenton

LA RIVIERE DE SEINE

Fargue taught us to sublimate everyday life and make the highest poetry out of it.
— Max Jacob

There is an unknown demon within Fargue that seems to drive him to the most audacious comparisons, in which he makes use of animals, cathedrals, or monsters to castigate the moral squalor of his day. It is a matter of pure poetry, an agility of spirit that leads him ceaselessly to find resemblances or associations for everything his eyes fall on.
— André Beucler

There are so many different individuals in Fargue, so many secrets, so many torturous byways, so many personalities (and each one of them so complex), that half a dozen critics would hardly suffice to sum him up.
— Edmond Jaloux

Nothing could be more astounding to me than Léon-Paul Fargue's "Horoscope" — Absurd, incongruous, touching, and nostalgic.
— Henry Miller

Fargue transforms reality & incites it to undergo perilous metamorphoses, and eventually drives it some way toward the abyss. That is the danger of an art devoted to metaphor: it calls everything into question; but that is also its merit, and in the lament for the life of another era which Fargue readily, too readily, intones, it is right that we should hear the wrong note, the unheard of note, which intrudes into it like the cracked echo of an enigma.
— Maurice Blanchot

LE PLAN DE LA VILLE, CITE, VNIVE

Chasteau de vincennes

Port S. Antoine

R. S. Estienne

La place Royalle

Marche du Temple

Fauxbourg S. Martin

S. Denis

S. Denis

les Halles

Les marets

La grage Bateliere

Ceste ville est un autre monde,
Dedans un monde florissant:
En peuple et en biens puissant,
Qui de toutes choses abonde.

Mathias Merian, Basiliense, fecit

Léon-Paul Fargue

High
Solitude

Léon-Paul Fargue

High
Solitude

Translated by Rainer J. Hanshe

Contra Mundum Press   New York · London · Melbourne

High Solitude
© 2024 Rainer J. Hanshe;
Haute Solitude
© 1941 Léon-Paul Fargue.

First Contra Mundum Press
edition 2024.

"Advocacy of Disorder" was
first featured in *Firmament*,
Vol. 1, № 3 (July 2021) 57–61,
"Leaning" in *minor literature[s]*,
«rentrée littéraire» (Sept 2024),
and "High Solitude" *&* "Azazel"
in *Vestiges*, 6 (Aug 2022) 82–97.
The translator expresses his
gratitude to Joshua Roothes,
Tobias Ryan, *&* Jared Fagen.

Library of Congress
Cataloguing-in-Publication
Data

Fargue, Léon-Paul,
1876–1947
High Solitude /
Léon-Paul Fargue

—1st Contra Mundum Press
Edition

220 pp., 5 × 8 in.

ISBN 9781940625706

  I. Fargue, Léon-Paul.
 II. Title.
III. Hanshe, Rainer J.
 IV. Translator.

2024937543

This publication has been
aided by support from
The Montparnasse Cultural
Foundation.

THE MONTPARNASSE
CULTURAL FOUNDATION

TABLE OF CONTENTS

… then were served…

… the happelourdes, the badigonyeuses, the étangourres, the aucbares of the sea, the godiveaulx de lévrier, biens bons, the bourbelettes, Primeronges, the bregizol- lons, the frelinginigues, the starabillatz, the cornicabotz, the cornamcuz revestuz de bize, the jerangoys, the mopsopige, the chinfreneaulx, the volepupinges, the ondre spondredetz, the friande vestanpenarderie, the bandyelivagues, viande rare, the notrodilles, the spo- pondrilloches, the ancrastabotz, the croquinpedaignes, the gringuenauldes à la joncade...

How the Lady Lanterns were served at supper.

Rabelais, The Fifth Book of the Good Pantagruel, XXXII bis.

I Dreamed

A poet who made a dream out of bounds
Told me that a star exists in a radiant sky
Where the brief hour never sounds
That hour when hearts break to say goodbye.
                    (From a song by Paul Delmet)

Up there, in that exclusive dimension, they were starting to realize that I wasn't quite at ease. I myself realized it.

I had been well received, like a slightly Zenoesque dreamer none too surprised by death.

But now I had manifested clear signs of anxiety. A scrap of a truncated idea, like the fore-end of a wasp that has been guillotined but which continues to groom and frenetically scour its legs, hummed again in my vitreous head.

I still tended to my limits, to gather myself within myself, to corset anew my chrysalis. A new man was coagulating.

My number, my old identification as a disintegrated person, was lengthened furtively into a patronymic capital letter. Hey! The monogram of the old man dodges God's conscription! The hopping insect tries to put itself back together ...

— Not so tired of living, they whispered, as to stir up so much existence...

— He will curdle the milk of the spheres.

— He's like those poorly neutered cats that still go prowling.

— Is he a revolutionary? Is he an overzealous bit player who does his best to create faux agitation?

— More than suspect...

— The metempsychosis had not taken hold. The dialyzer didn't have much effect...

— Should we light the hand of glory?

— Let those who sleep, sleep. Let those who are awake remain awake...

— But look at him, he's slipping away! grumbled the silent voices of the ether...

The Sanhedrin drew nearer, grouped itself in steps, like a large, well-planned meal, closely followed by the serving trays. The divine parties began to ring, clashing with crystal words of princely familiarity. A Mexican god, a block of obsidian with heaven-laden eyes, made of mountain and rain powers, came to my defense.

I was carrying on before great multi-valved shells with prehensile eyes like leeches, crowned with prismatic tiaras, reflectors, and deforming mirrors polluted by love, desiccated by disciples, ravaged by exegesis, bohued but always august and sufficiently garnished with wisdom and the usual objects, which decided at any event, in short, to purge me in the mode of some permission given to the Earth, with a diversion through mutual agreement of the temporal and the spiritual, obligatory intelligence with a guarantee of the Eternal, the periscope for internal use, the ability to see without being seen, facing the transparent side of the glass we call "the sun" (the other side of which is a mirror depicting an imbecile), and all license to move yourself in time as well as in space.

They concluded with a breath of emotion. But the mystics are ptosic and the gods ærophagous...

— Vomit finally with a lucid heart and die knowingly! And report everything back to us. Cordially.

So here I am descending then, like an extra-lucid parachute, gliding along the erg with its adorable filigree, moiré like a squid-god, through the sacred whitenesses and albuginous trails...

I can already feel the eternal gradually fading, stretching a lot, cracking, bending, like a "gauge" in a kiln.

Stupendous. Here we go, now I'm talking to myself.

This space and this material, the resolutions, the appoggiatura, the incredible striae, the indefinitely relative and complementary palette that men so greatly ignored, my descending water pipe has a completely new sense of it.

... But what is this ghostly-shaft that rises, parallel to me like the counterweight of an elevator?

I recognize myself fairly well. I find, so I think, by the left hem, what I saw in the past when I climbed the right hem, along a vertical candle, draped over the glimmer, which resembles my memory, and which my magick lantern sends in the plumage of night ...

I can better see his face, and I realize that on his forehead he bears the Stygmann de la Luçâze! ...

... It's true, it's difficult to speak and to touch. It still requires a great deal of precautions. As soon as I touch it with my head, newly sharpened from the battle, everything is recast in the divine ...

From time to time a muted star, playing a blocked horn, a glassy tiger that rattles on the edge of the abyssal bell and which my old soul brushes with a sad comb, lets loose, from the depths of a rumor smoked through space, a kind of pink bark that comes from a hundred billion centuries and beasts, and again slowly passes the scrutiny of death ...

Because I've brushed up against it, that, that is mine, yes, I have often come close, I want to know at what moment of its duration, of its methods and of its love, I had come close to the extreme point of some terrible life, rolled up in some very old style, spawn of an old cosmic espadon, carried by an old cat-like planet, in love with too many masters, which bristled and softly mewed in the ether, like a plaintive voice wavering in a dying man's room badly illuminated by the swell of rooftops...

This time, I can feel it; I'm entering the zone. I perceive, as far as the ground level stretches, vast expanses colored with grief...

I hear thunder beneath me, like a great dreaming beast turning in its sleep. Finally! Something alive!

Let loose by degrees from my descending water pipe, I grope around. And, I've chosen the wrong epoch, naturally.

I arrive just above the secondary epoch: the Jurassic period. Such is my luck.

Help! I thought. Well... Forgive me! I'm not used to it yet...

I plant myself at the peak, in a dreadful stench of coal, peat, and old oyster, twenty yards from two giant saurians that clash with fury. They trumpet like a hundred thousand haunted caves, with their horseshoe-like jaws. They look like two grottoes of Staffa molars. Great wads of slime and phlegm rain down on me almost continually. And it smells of firestone, tar, dirty belly, day-old cadavers, green dung! The thunderstorm caulks the blue shells of monstrous mushrooms and crests, with dizzying threads of electric hailstones, the leaflets of surtarbrandur that stomp along the horizon!

... No! I loved all that when I was burning for Natural History and reading Zimmerman's books and thought I saw flowing, in the sails of my poor window, the great blink of the eye, the great call of diluvian light. Am I meant to never see them again, should I quench that passion only in death? Not like that, no, not like that! No mirage in time! Not now! That's not what I'm looking for. I must win back my own history.

Forthwith, there is a fading of dimensions. I oscillate a bit in the noises and sulfurous slings, like a little boat shaken by the wake of an offshore vessel.

I sway, once the terrestrial equation makes its claim, between the zenith and the nadir, and I take off again into that mortal sadness which itself breathes.

Soon, I see grains in the sky, winged beechnuts … Here then are my brothers and their weight …

Finally, I start to skip old cuttlebones from a tower, a dome, a roof, a belfry. I approach, trembling, the signs that they were writing, the iron loaves that they were kneading, the stone fruits that they made to ripen so as to furnish their sonorous heads, alone for so long on a vigil, with sooty whiskers, whitened with guano, riddled, wrinkled by distracted waters, trampled, hollowed out by burning feet and soaked with spectres, spying on each other, slowly blinking with the grimy lashes of their nocturnal dials, and which heard so few words …

... I will have slipped from level to level, until I can smell the breath of the streets, the belly and the scorched sex of houses, stuffed with commodities and caches, the toothless mouths of doors, windows, shops, in the grumble of metallic grills, pumps, and works drenched in the great angry rumor. And I get a foothold in the backwash of scolopendromorphs ...

I find shuddering the murmur of a rising street, the backs of passersby who stop and breathe slyly against one another and who secretly goad each other, like insects. From time to time, I see through the transparency, in its limestone and fibrin coat-rack, the kit of a man, the red egg for darning stockings, the fluted chalk sponge, the well-cut salt of a sacred organ, caught in a tight net of manias ...

But what troubles and brings me closer? I was bouncing off the walls ...

I soar above the family tomb, with its chapel and its little stained-glass windows, whose blue eyes make me tremble.

And I see ascending, by ropes, a sort of large pencil box that is followed by a black-clad monomaniac.

It's curious, I can't, from above, turn away from that pencil box that seems to mean so much to me? And I lose nothing in the distance.

... A bit higher in the time that sucks me up and continues to assail me, but slowly and gently.

... I see, before a dilapidated window and on a high marble fireplace, a small and very old copper coffee pot. And then, it's him, my cat, there he is! with his arms crossed, coiled on the shelf, in the midst of all sorts of bric-a-brac. He watches, as my mother used to say, he watches his sweeties passing in the street ...

That's it — I'm clinging to my life! It's my room! Nothing to do but follow.

... But my room is illuminated at night by my poor ceiling lights, the last memories of the little studio that we had in the suburbs ... Everything is half-lit. And in the corners, and on the chairs, and on the couch, and in the corridor, shadows gaze at the ground and won't let me see their faces. And I see at last in my bed, drawing my horse-blanket, I see, with a movement of shame and the greediest curiosity, a severe body that smells of wood, the finally fixed plasticine face, finally hardened, which life had long and lovingly worked to death ...

So, my God, who was waiting for me in my shallows, because he doesn't like lyricism, and he doesn't want our soul to be held by the great words we have made for it ...

— Stop complaining, he says. The last hour is the one when the dish is ready to be eaten. When you opened your mouth a bit and made the little movement that separated you from yourself, you almost reduced the aroma of your soul. And an entire lifetime isn't enough to prepare such a meal. Friends, you are good cooks, and I am not a bad chef. Stop then being afraid of ghosts …

— I was the one who brought you back, since you wished to live again, and not the foolish demons that made an ass of you in your nightmare. Once, I saw you take a woman out of the oven. Today, I saw you take a house out of the oven. I have always followed you in spite of yourself; I have always loved you in spite of myself, since the day you were taken out of a little box from a patch of sky. You couldn't do a thing for your loss. Wake up; come back to me, come back to us, let's go up together. Don't try to understand too much. And I'll tell you something …

— Go down a bit more into your box before we leave again.

I obeyed the Master's voice and found myself in a workshop of ceramicists singing under the ghost of my father.

Heave-ho! God threw me the rope. And my entire life rose before me.

Prehistoric Visitation

... In the great nebulous spinning-top, from where Trimurti will stick out his big amiable Cerberus head in the center of a vast coquemar circled with light and shadow, the cosmic plasma condensed itself to secrete this black sweat: Men.

Men were carried away from floor to floor by the cataract of the epochs toward Death, since the first adventure of Worlds!

... The sun left the scoriaceous film with the speed of a champagne cork. Then, the teetotums turned less strongly. The warm-hearted stones assumed their uniform. The fists of darkness relaxed, tired from churning gold and bitumen. The music of the spheres raised its white hand. The great leading roles of a gelatinous opera were grouped on a rotating stage 40,000 kilometers in equatorial circumference, the atmosphere, the lithosphere, the Goulfe, the Moropiate, Cape Horn, which has the graces of the pucrasia, limestone blocks with their ptychozoon-parachute heads, bournonite in cumbersome frocks, granitic elephants, curved and black like Bretons at a funeral.

At the call of a pure and senseless voice, the steam held back its terrible rocket. The ghosts assembled, the figures listened, and, at an Argentinian command, the suns playing thanksgiving with Death leaped radiantly to their order of battle along the celestial curves. Kneaded, rolled, rejected, reabsorbed, revomited by a thronging crowd of cloud-cannons and artillery showers, silicon, sodium, manganese, dust, radium, and mud imbricated in the puzzle.

In the shadow where the voices were spaced out, we heard the muffled hatching, one after another, of archipelagoes. The Earth cracked open its fire-belching grenade. Volcanoes bled in the screeching water. The feldspar went in search of its Massif. The porphyries struck like simooms, choosing red for the Latin world, blue for the Nile Valley. Cut into slices, like pineapples, the basalts proposed models of amphitheaters and cathedrals. And from every side thundered the sledgehammers of the invisible construction site of the gods.

Then, when sweetness had gradually insinuated itself into the brawl, like a woman uttering a specious right, when the puff pastry of the clays was cooked through, when the slates of the Ardennes and the sands of the Kalahari had received their patents of spontaneous invention, when the brains of puddingstone had coiled like necklaces in a torrent, the Silurian seas ceased to waltz, spread out, and began their somber pregnancy.

A huge minium sun quivered in a sky of lead. Fires broke out like lava. Vines of liquid fire whipped the dough of the newborn. The seething waters trickled over the young skin of the world, causing explosions of talc and geysers of sweat, seeking the smallest pockets, thimbles, pores, folds, grotto keyholes, the hollow teeth of quarries, dripping on varnished undulations, accumulating ton by ton, tear by tear, in the wrinkles of a face howling with heat, leaping on the spasms of a globe drunk with abscesses, covered with chemical leprosy, swollen with mountains of black pus.

It rained at 360° on sentimental rocks, the pain of which can be measured, in our pitiful days, by the convulsions of lobsters cooked American style and truite au bleu, which they have kept from this turnaloonesque and ropatorted cooking.

Rock faces sprouted like flowers. The first dreams of the Earth were rustling. Mucosal lamps ignited and began their journeys. The first animated cartoons ran on ladders of rainwater that adorned the fireball with crystal hair. Eddies of broth threw polyp beefsteaks on the first ribs, and marsh pastries on hills sans vertebrae. The barley gruel of shellfish was deposited in the depths of the sea. Limestone festivals were being organized. And coral concerts were already celebrating the birthday of the sun, the tercentenary of plasma, the jubilees of wind, din, and color.

Vaginas of pitch, peat, and coal began to open. Late aeroliths sometimes flattened into cow dung on new plateaus. Santa heads appeared in the windows of Jurassic limestone libraries. Pterichthys settled into the gelatinous depths. Terrain and forests emerged like demodex. Hairy and barbarous toys were amassed before the escarpments. The first snow fell. And the first snow disappeared, sweetening the lakes, filling with liquors the rivers that began to flow. Invisible jewelers went to work on chains, cut needles, disposed garlands in the Straits of Gibraltar, imposed the Himalayas on the world, polished the tabular architectures of Brazil to the bone. The forms of life, massed in ranks like troops in a meeting, awaited the signal.

Then, a giant toad sounded its horn in the twilight of the marshlands. The cement was hard. Chandeliers of stars announced that the Earth was ready. The Laurentian Plateau rose like an elevated trail. The Allegheny Mountains took the lead in the parade. Scotland appeared. Artillery and deep-sea ironworks were making the first rings of the animal kingdom. The first eyes, the first cheeks of the world, began to live in the aftertaste of the seas: paradoxides resembling piano bellies, jousting harnesses, coats of arms of coral caves, artichoke-worms, arthropods and brachiopods of the first days, which astonished the genii of the water by their dignity as battleship turrets, their bonhomie as harmonicas, their jaw-legs and their lung-legs. Billions of worm-kids, baby-asidaspises, woodlice forefathers swirled in underwater ironworks: typewriter-hedgehogs, radiators, siphon-insects, vaporizer-leeches, mustache bolts, corkscrew-crabs, eyeless eyelashes, enormous & tiny metazoans, abdomen-shaped towers, pyramid-crustaceans, locomotive-lobsters soaked in creator juice and reproduced without muddle. Thus the seas were peopled with fabulous vermin, for the waters perfected the fruits of the heat ...

From the earth that was drying like a building smeared with sperm, long stretches of smoke rose as far as the eye could see, grouped in geysers of green stars. The sigillaria raised their hairy strobiles. And prodigious trees partitioned the sky with their canopies, like a greenhouse intoxicated with light and silence. The great saurians, covered in greasy and bright-colored scales, imbricate themselves, leaping like storm-battered marsupials, with two thousand teeth and bird feet, fought in the sonorous grottoes, opening huge unpleasant mouths.

The arsinotherium, which was lugging an obelisk between its eyes, waded through the horsetail puree of a swampland that might be Alexandria, Sucre, Edinburgh, or the Marennes. Frail and crooked plants broke like cathedrals of crockery. In the beards of young indigo, lemon, or wine-colored mountains, convoluted cucumbers and eared mushrooms frolicked in a moss able to twist up into spirals and give birth to emerald caterpillars.

Long as balustrades and graceful as viaducts, thirsty insects suddenly detached themselves from a squadron, landed, emptied a pond in one go, and flew away, its noise like that of a traveling circus. Stinkbugs pissed ink on algae. The slightest wind sent whole fleets of trees flying, the debris of which was scattered like pollen over cities of polypods and fortresses of lichen. The torrents were working on future coals.

A perfumed moon created freshwater phantoms, made vegetal apparitions run, and presaged the spectres of giraffes and the spirits of mirrored armoires in that setting which makes me want to cry, which pains me with regret, in this soulless and godless decor, in this carboniferous or Jurassic forest, the lost paradise of monsters...

Then came the hour of the first revolution: that of exuberance. An inaugural spring saw growing on the motionless globe golden trees and asparagus with transparent tiaras. Mountains of lace were reflected around the sudden Tethys. Madrepore casinos and coniferous caravans were established. Already, the ammonites were thinking of capitals, stairways, arenas. Poplar and viburnum-eating reptiles gave pause before flowers. Arcaded dragons promenaded the armored train of their tails over nicotine beaches and deposited barbed droppings from which floated seahorses lithe as tapeworms and turbine tadpoles.

Marabout-horses galloped between the legs of a Brontosaurus...

Insect wars broke out at great heights. The Ichthyosaurus and the Plesiosaurus slept like old cannons along the oily rivers of the polybius henslowii. The shadow of the Diplodocus cast night over the continents of anthills, disturbing the standards of the termite world. The Dinocéras and the Machairodus dreamed of Museums, Gobelins, steel- and glass-covered station halls. Telescope fish and phyllimorphes with propellers suddenly met like two rapids, knotted together, soused each other with molten lead, green blood, and burst after a week of fighting in a fracas of explosive eggs. From their putrid ashes sprang a new monster, shining like armor, swimming in the air and evaporating with the skillful art of a will-o'-the-wisp.

The Pterodactyls, birds of Lake Stymphale and vampires of Kansas planted themselves on the rocks like soft axes or cleaved the sky with a crooked gesture, striking the air with the dry blows of their iron beaks. The carnivorous Goulaphon clambered through the lonely forests. The iguanodon was waiting for him without laughing, at the end of some crossroads, perched on a green light, hoping to battle him with his terrible thumb-horn. Strange beasts, covered with a populous riffraff, peeled off the bark of trees as they scratched their backs bristling with scimitars. And the great Serpent of the Sea had already come to walk its endless melancholy in the warm basin of the Seine.

The chirping of ugly birds sounded everywhere, the breathing of rhinos seeded with nails, the hissing of motionless stones, white-hot from the tertiary sun and which suddenly started to gallop, false turtles pretending to be roads, flat crocodiles the color of trench coats mocked the blue zebras by being sidewalks. Sometimes, a husky yelp was blasted skyward, announcing the killing of an ostrich or a scarab in the linoleum bush, or the arrival on the beach of some hatted fish from which wheels emerged once it ran out of water. And yet, nothing was closer to silence than the clamors of the young world where nightmare existed in its purest state!

But in this world of five-legged rhododendrons, of heavy birds adorned with telegraph wires and surmounted with eye-pallets, in the wake of smoldering pachyderms that moved as slowly as churches, along the forests of iodine and snow-plows where skeletons hung like fruits, among giant spiders, humped with horns, heavy with breasts, in the calm of the first blond dew, the first vapors, the first typhoons, timid as a gazelle, awkward, inoffensive, and cowardly, a bizarre Monster would sometimes appear, more of a machine than an animal, almost a construction, something uniquely developed and uniquely stupid, a solemn mixture of fine beast and podagra bird, a successful plant, perfectly vulnerable and perfectly desirable, an enemy of everything, emitting cries, seeking quarrels, incapable of speed, precision, patience, flair, ignorant of the winds, dying young, sickly, cross-eyed, industrious & melancholic: Man.

... And then the sky grew softer. The pastures bluish. The mastodon appeared slowly along the hillocks, like an immense leather vessel, shaking in the sun its ears all ringing with parasites. Potassons, depopotamuses, and dilepotheses will emerge from the rivers while opening the organ grinder's jalopy-like jaws. The hipparion leaped about on a meadow, curved like an ancient horse, and the monkeys began to unwind along the trees. Made dreamy by the panthers, by a zebu sad as an old forgotten minister, by goupule trees, by their juicy pictoles, man sometimes envisaged the dog, the cat, the dandelion, the silkworm, the swallowtail, the scarab, and the carrier pigeon...

And I was warned by my childish senses, groping through the darkness of the epochs, and I sensed that the hand of the gods slyly molded some tremulous marvel among the baleen plates and the grimaces and would some day bring forth, for my pleasures, a vermilion wave, pure as an almond emerging from its pod, under the canopy of a dawn that would make the World a Room of Love, and like a thing so perfect

that it would make you cry nervously or yearn to
degrade and worship her, oh! to beat and to kiss her,
Venus Anadyomene ...

Sometimes, I woke up in a deafened world, a child-
old man surprised by a change of scenery in favor of
man. The Pekinese had replaced the terebellid. The
streetcars were losing steam, compared to the flying
dragons of my civilization. Secondary. The dirigibles
seemed useless and uncertain to me. Finally, no longer seeing trees, plants, or breathing the scents of
the natural world, I blushed, to find myself where
I was, to have survived so long after the end of my
Old World ...

So, I began to think of the joy of travelers, of ex-
plorers, of the discoverers of deserts, of waterfalls,
of mines, of sailors or poets. I was thinking of this
little-known painter, beloved by Delacroix, the painter Catlin, who wrote a precious little book, noticed
by Baudelaire and which was re-published in the
Bibliothèque Rose as a New Year's book. I think of
Stevenson, of Paul Gauguin, of Joseph Conrad, who
had the joy, the long joy of being able to evade their
disgust.

Yet that joy, that illusion of regaining the Lost
World, I experienced it one day just as they had. At
a very young age, I came to the shores of poetry, and

the welcoming ground of an unknown land suddenly traveled beneath my feet ... One day, on the arm of my father, I discovered that lyrical universe, all vibrating with echoes: at the Jardin des Plantes.

It seemed to me that day like a Paradise Found, a paradise otherwise splendid and which gradually reopened, calm, in my memory. The period was also calm, propitious ... The caretaker of the Museum evoked the seriousness of a granitic rock. The animals were well nourished, though disappointed by the paucity of man's imagination, he who had lived so many years just to take on constraints, uniforms, debts, wars. In the cage of his kiosk, military music bellowed crudely. Soldiers of that time resembled penguins and flamingoes, the lotuses and the birches of my dreams. Stiff Kepi, red pants, in the note of the number 1 outfit of Berrichon and Jurassic butterflies, Oligocene ladybugs. The nurses wore broad bonnets, with long dangling ribbons, known as "Follow Me Young Man," and which had the shape of a finned Saint-Honoré. The Jardin des Plantes was part of the Sunday oasis. It was quiet and beatific, and made me nostalgic for snow and bear carnivals, sea lions and Ice Age mica plains ...

Since then, there have been hard, hungry periods, deluges and chaos ... A lack of money. A dilapidated garden as after a tornado or the passage of a vengeful diplodocus preserved in the alcohol of a volcano.

The animals were malnourished, sad. Melancholy articles appeared in the newspapers. Then came the gradual decline, the abandon that came with war.

Around 1912, the Jardin d'Acclimatation presented a kind of circulating exhibition where we saw exhibited, in boxes and in display cases installed by someone who had a sense of pleasant disorder, strange fish, which made my Old World childhood heart leap. Faux-fish, swallow-fish, elegant monsters of the seas of China in the form of horn combs, bizarre croissants, or musical instruments, chainmail hurdy-gurdys, haggard-eyed rebecs, reductions of harps, carved in cymophane...

There were also insects, beetles, and Lepidoptera, at all stages of their evolution, from birth to rage, from egg to revolution behind glass vitrines. The guards kept an eye on the cocoons, as if they were the inconsistent and flabby jewels of Prehistory. Every day I witnessed the spectacle of their metamorphoses. A beetle emerged from its organic funnel all coal-black, unwound itself in the air and fluted in golden colors. Night butterflies, the Acherontia atropos, the death's head Sphinx, were undressing themselves, unsheathing, as if from a suit, out of their chrysalis into a mahogany waistcoat, all wrinkled, still all wet. Me, I had time... A barely perceptible voice warned me that I was in the presence of a mystery whose purity had been unsullied for centuries *&* centuries by any refinement. I stopped for a long time to see the butterflies gradually stretch out over the ribs of their bodices, like little velvet fans, and dry in the sun. Finally, I gazed attentively at the Tsetse fly, dark as a slumbering seed, cautiously enclosed in its little crystal flask...

If I dwell on this exhibition, it is because it was for me a very small documentary of the great freedom of crawling or flying peoples in the first moments of the globe. Since then, the "Vivarium" has been created to extend its conquest and give asylum to the numerous emigrants of the lands subject to man: caterpillars, bees, and grasshoppers. It is there that giant beetles, black as catafalques, pace the ground of their meager prison. They extend a long barbed paw, a veritable harpoon, to tickle the noses of large mygalomorphae spiders, which, like spinning tops, snort through their freckles. Everyone is mixed together: compsognathus' in reduction, lucani joined to tangles of lizards, centrote omelets bristling with hatpins.

In an angelica-colored box, small shrubs are seen where, slyly clinging and stuck together, the dry-leaf phyllies and phasmids, Devil's sticks, imitate branches and leaves so closely that they provoke fear. Further on, in the apartments of snakes, coral elaps resemble an ear of bad corn. The Vivarium is a treasury of obscure and brilliant passions...

I find myself cast back to a distant time. I can surmise the feelings of war, the astonishment and joy of primitive man. I return to the pleasures and enthusiasms of an age without memory when children were not children, but young monsters, who had only natural wonders to play with.

... What skeleton rests, in the depths, under this statue? What millennium-old powder do the roots of this plane tree drink up? What robust and naked beach once stretched out in place of this streetcar cage where the bourgeois women of the suburbs crowd today, their pants glued to their buttocks and their armpits black with new insects invented through the centuries of myelitis and of machines that make mutton-chops? What trilobite with movable binding, founder of the order of lobsters, inventor of contoured shells, has counted its legs on those layers of moss that today are plumbed by the long sadness of a barracks?

I hurry over this debris, jostling pure-eyed public servants with flageolet complexions, well-born bourgeois who wallow amongst booksellers so as to perfect their general culture and therefore be able to resist via their heads the organization of the proletarian hordes, Modern Fronts that threaten fragile cities, forests of azaleas, swimming pools, the solfataras of swimmers, similar to a charge of brontosauri, horizontal Eiffel towers, moving temples,

bas-reliefs on stilts, crenelated walls of thirty tons
that would have demolished oaks and menhirs with
a blow of the tail ...

On my return home, I threw myself into the Devo-
nian darkness, as one throws oneself into the water.
I implored the carboniferous nightmare ... Little by
little, a square disappeared under the pressure of
pentacrines, sigillaria, and gymnosperms of fossil
botany. The docks of Canal Saint Martin gave way
to red sandstone lagoons where the semaphore
Dinornis, the giant Moa of New Zealand, trotted at
140 kilometers an hour, covering with ocher dust
the South American armadillos with embroidered
carapaces, damascened like Arabian saddles, and
which remained in place, like the cupolas of an en-
trenched camp. On its legs, a grand piano ending in
a large bulldog head, its neck stuffed with a greased
buoy, the Plesiosaurus revolved around the quaternary mammoth, so badly shaved, so sorry to have to
appear everywhere preceded by those huge tusks ...

The obtuse Stegosaurus, borer of tunnels, all
bristling with railway company disc plates and
as if armed with anti-aircraft instruments, sawed,
bit, used trees, and watched them fall, spitting a
sword-swallowing laugh at the boarding schools of
ferns out for a walk. Here is the deer with antlers

built for bomber planes, the pelor-umbrella, the ceritium-tiara, the steno-dactyl, for which I have grown old with questions ... In my half-slumbering head, half-mad to surrender to those epochs when life was so abundant that the dust of animals and insects was used to make stone, a scorpion whirlpools in the sand ...

A classic pendulum strikes the hour in the 10th arrondissement. Not an eyelid moves. The neighborhood sleeps; the neighborhood can sleep. Men have died of fatigue and indifference. Some old man is watching, however. I see his window. Big butterflies kill themselves at will trying to cross through windows, not knowing that, if the glass yielded, they would return to some bulb, hot as the first stew of the world, where the promises of trees were cooking with indecisive wingless bacilli and asterophyllites ...

What scenes unraveled in the place where you have your room, where you dreamed under the lamp and tempered your forehead in your hands? A monster was snoring there under the sea ...

And in these streets, and in these places, you pass on the arm of a friend, your voice echoing in the night, and you are reconstructing the world, and the gaze of the dead stars only reaches us today ...

But the world isn't that bad, and it is empty. The sun is 8 light minutes from earth, the first star 4 years old, the Andromeda Nebula 1 million, & those little blue splinters that I barely notice are billions of years away. The world is neither old nor young anymore, it is expanding. My fossil loves, my not yet unearthed cretaceous monsters, will explode with the plasma. The nebulae disperse. The further away they are from us, the faster they seem to go. Thus we hear, at a height higher than its real height, the whistle of the Orient Express, which passes in a whirlwind before us, while the stars are dying ...

What cosmogonic hypothesis could very simply give us this lost world: peace of heart? O small world, whose telescopes can reach a hundred million years, what tiny place do you occupy in the fictive intensity of the void? And as for the primitive ages of matter, there is nothing left of them but waves ...

Alarm Clock

Alarm clock on standby. A gentle voice: Do you want to have lunch? Flick of the switch. The green basin rolls a wave toward the plaster sky. Verses from Banville leap into the arena:

The green sea where the waves bristle,
The sea of tumultuous waves, the sea ...

Straightaway, stripes! Entering into the round. The spray of the street, the rotating song of trucks, the blue rattle of an engine that never ceases to leave, leaves falsely, is forgotten, then recast on me from the end of the horizon, the veiled drums of the open sea conjure me, the horn of a fire engine urges me on.

"Here's your mail." Troubled reading. Browsing through the newspaper. Falling back into sleep.

... You know it's 10 o'clock? I count again to 20, on the nape of my neck, the pillow well raised so that my head does not touch the wall. Two or three turns to the left, which casts my eye on the teeth of the little clock. And, let's go! Dressing gown.

Now it's trotting time for an apartment horse. I hear another next door. The house begins to knock. The corridor creaks. My cat gently pushes the door open, stretches out and yawns, looks at me, speaks briefly, and leaps on the table. "Oh, what is it boooo, my lion has to pee-pee." But it's time to recount his sorrows — they call for help from the depths of our eyes, from the depths of the city, and lo and behold that idiot sneezes in my face while I'm on the phone. It's the effect it has on him. I know someone who's going to get demoted. Punished by the window!

Lunch. Tea with milk. In vain I say that I will not make too thick a sandwich. Kief for the first cigarette.

Corridor. The bathroom is never-ending. Stubborn, stiff, somnambulic lathering. Here begins the drama.

Visonin, the first name of Visu (nature).

When dressing myself, I put on ghosts haunted by malice. In our absence, clothes are regained by their demons, which sometimes let themselves be surprised. Our loves are maniacs. Handle the shirt, passing the left sleeve, well placed, so as not to tear the hanging thread of an always-possible spider. To button the collar, raise it wide, taking some space, still not snagging anything, and push the button into its eyelid in one fell swoop. Put the boxer shorts on the axis, too, because by putting the foot too far inside or too far out it could be forced into the oblique folds and into the seams, and once again drive out the threads of the virgin washerwoman. (Oh, these threads, he imagines that by passing his foot through, he will puncture an entire network ... Seeing threads everywhere? Wouldn't it be like seeing rats every-

where, as alcoholics do? But he is not an alcoholic.
So? Abulia, bad scruples, mental confusion, feverish
anxiety?) Then, stretch the silk over the leg. Adjust
the socks a bit far and straight, because they could
get a bit askew and the little toe would be misplaced,
which cannot be put back, if it is crumpled. Put your
shoes on straight, pull the flap and untwist the laces
taking care to even them out. (Not convenient.)

Brush the back of your suspenders, and pass them
wide over the head, so as not to snag wild hair, which
would have to be pulled and broken …

Same care as above to get into the pants. The haz-
ardous thread, or the garters, could snag buttons, fabric, hair, and stretch other tender threads that would
suspend and gather its fall, and which would have
to be broken again, against all rules of equilibrium
and correction. The same game for the vest openings.

Thrust the tie down into the false collar so that,
if it is of a very flexible fabric, it emerges, gradually,
from the left, and does not get caught between the
collar and the shirt and on the skin — unpleasant
sensation.

Very neat execution of the tie knot, always wide,
to avoid pulling threads, taking care that the corselet
of the evening cravat is well placed.

Wide application of the jacket collar on the nape
of the neck, taking it from a distance, for the same
reasons as above. The rest to match.

Brush the jacket by stretching the folds vertically, to avoid horizontal dust streaks.

Careful brushing of the bottom of the pants, because the brush dragged a bit when passing over it, with an inclusive gesture ...

Item for the bottom of the overcoat, a lasso made of dust and of sheep wool.

Last polishing of the shoes, which, along with this entire struggle, may have picked up something.

Last helping hand to straighten the collars, tuck in the shoulders, straighten the fronts.

A worried, prolonged gaze to see if I'm forgetting anything, on the fireplace or on the table. This woad, placed upright on the marble, inclines its wrinkled golden forehead. Push the statuette, or the small old kettle, against it. Wind the clock, which turns back when it isn't necessary. Nudge that book that slips to the edge of the desk.

Leave the room with all sorts of precautions, regret, and repentance, tightening the buttocks and covering oneself with the extended left arm, in order to avoid throwing a cigarette spark or ashes on the horse blanket of the sofa bed.

As much the same thing in the corridor, because the wardrobe is as crowded as at Bluebeard's.

The windows, on all sides, look at me, look at one another, whisper, dream in their shirts, play ghost, drink a color, say mass at the altar opposite, with naked arms cooing and recovering themselves, to the heat's rose, to the smoked glass of a cloud.

Departure.

If it's noon, descend toward Gare de l'Est, my bakery of memories ...

Then, I walk along large dark buildings with sky in between, often solitary, lit in broad daylight, in the midst of which sails a tiny square with a statue of a seated woman who weeps and prays for me, for my old suburb, for my destroyed house, for the tempted soul of Gare de l'Est.

Secret Geography

But has the importance of the viscera, which is indispensable to social life, and which the ancients might have deified, been well examined? Speculator, you build a neighborhood, or even a village; you have built more or fewer houses, you have been daring enough to erect a church; you find some kind of inhabitants, you pick up a pedagogue, you hope for children; you have made something that has the air of a civilization, like making a pie: there are mushrooms, chicken feet, crayfish and dumplings; a presbytery, deputies, a rural guard and administrators: nothing will hold, everything will dissolve, unless you have united this microcosm with the strongest of social bonds, with an épicier.

— Honoré de Balzac, "The Épicier"

When very young, this beautiful piece made me want to write. The fact, too much proved by my concierge, who then resembled a vitelotte, that society, even the smallest, one that would fit in a jalopy or Jew's harp, owed the mystery of its starting up and the oils of its smooth operation to a bakery, worked at me at night like an erotic dream and penetrated deeply into my imagination. I could no longer hold my head high and my hands behind my back before the shops of Bardou, Lecat, and Mancel, or of Father Samigre, our sugar and bay leaf supplier, without telling myself that this man, a big-bellied Morvandiau with cauliflower ears, had a vested interest in the Last Judgment. Sentences strike you like this, carving out an immense void in your heart on which women have not yet drunk. There was still, a bit further along, on Boulevard Magenta, yet another épicier, one called Fondayr, the son of a rust remover from Beirut, who was lounging, his eyes lower than his nostrils, before his ship. He was a fellow with a nose crooked and always full of bird-shot, with a Scottish mouth, all shriveled with bile and envy, a tear in his eye because of a fly that you pointed out to him in his barley cream, and a hand in the pocket to lend you six *sous* when you had no change when the tram would arrive; a poor bachelor stuck to the toes of his stepmother, envious of other people's wives, a crooked, grief-grating, liver-dammed, wound-digger, a sort of borborygmic snail whose hands I dared not shake. When I returned home, it took me long hours to tear myself away from that birdlime man, that pygmy dust that society needed to stay on its feet. Those two men, who had been dead in split peas for a number of years, opened doors for me, took me, if I must confess everything, by the hand, and threw me onto the tracks of an unknown city.

Far from looking, like Father Hugo, for the mental capers and beautiful storms out of which books are written, I suspect the two épiciers in my neighborhood, on whose track Balzac had thrown me, are not strangers to the research that I afterwards undertook in the bellows of the eyeless streets, along the quays dead with fear between the soft claws of the rivers, in all the frantic drama of the endless days of this enormous, heartless city where the ghosts of those who are no longer good for anything but sobbing in the depths of my soul await me.

This secret geography is the rather turbulent story of my tragic returns between my shadow and myself toward the tendernesses of a house that is no more, as toward this hotel with long legs, with mirrors, which welcomes the first escapees from myself toward the grey sky of the fever-jostled sleepless sheets. It's my tour as a police officer between the gas lights, it's the heartache of market gardeners at five in the morning, the trucks bending over the meat of the Halles like jungle phenomena, it's all the love and all the disgust of the saunterer whom I encounter, deprived of hope and solidity, when 6 A.M. strikes, when one begins to confuse vagabonds and revelers, stars and tail lights, men and beasts, wheels and wailings.

This geography has only one in-depth field of study: the Plutonism of Paris, the origénie of Gare de l'Est, Gare du Nord, Montmartre, and Bercy, the special constitution of des Enfants-Rouges, the cut of the earth's crust which sleeps like a drunkard off the coast of Montparnasse, the smut of sex tunnels, the faces of sad snobs, the great Insurance Company swindlers, the fencing hall chameleons, and a whole accumulation of more or less well-born, well-harnessed women, with stork-bill seed in the heart and morels in the brain. This whole diagram of monsters and of hypocrisy, of low thighs and greasy holy knives forms the backdrop.

For the man who wants to take the trouble, as for the good poet with the right shoes, Paris is a curious city, which has its folds, its ruptures, its broken down areas, its thrust sheets and its volcanism. There are neighborhoods that put pillows under your knees when you have sex with friendly women; neighborhoods that pour sleep-laden beers over you and where you fall asleep as if you were going to die. There are neighborhoods with bridles, neighborhoods haunted by ghosts, winged ichneumons as big as giraffes, streets that explode like the larva of stegomyia, crossroads filled with passersby who cling to houses like phasmids, dead ends encumbered with orthoptera, juicy plants where the foot cries out in despair, to others that are foamed up with French literature, the easy love of politicians and bar dramas; neighborhoods that smell of meat, glue, leather, yoghurt, labor, or nettles. Others, finally, where hurried souls run one after the other under the soles of the police, where one sees sheep and angels, the old carcasses of beggars with patched legs, baskets of sentiments, the limbs of kids and the holes of hell.

That whole unique eruption, which I had visited for years, entered my body. And as Balzac saw an épicier in the geometric location of all the commercial branches, I imagined a quadratic, debonair god, all leafy with scales and pinecones, a human tree, a sort of Cocagne mast, an Eiffel Tower switchbox that commands the muscles and spasms of Paris.

There remains the climate, the sky, the moderating role of clean and pious hearts, the temperature of stations and of parks, the cyclones and monsoons that whirl in the clubfooted boiler whose nocturnal caresses make the roots of our hair stiffen under our skulls. Ah! if you awaken at the opposite end of that black pole, you find yourself lying on the edge of a new and fresh city, all scintillating with fish without fishermen, virgin grasses, and fresh-faced kids! How often, when I walked among the wilds and the torrents of the places where I was led, I do not know by which derelict demons, how many times have I wished for the punch of the tumbling slate, the overstuffed car that takes a left, the terrestrial fistula that would have saved me from frozen and mouthless mornings. Then, I would have woken up between the curtains of a decapitated sun, in the tragic and silent charm of the landscapes of the afterlife, red with hope and calm under the machines of the heart.

But glaciers of fear and of madness pushed me onward every day, aged me every moment. I didn't see too many smiles forming on all the faces that my road had thrown at me since leaving high school. Cherished faces, friends and charming souls had been absorbed by squalid bellies even before all the words of affection I had prepared could have been said. I was, in that desert of churches, almost deprived of a torso and of fresh water, still walking at the head of the flock of my bones and my shadows, my legs lost and my fingers astray. All the flowers of Paris were springing up and turning yellow, governments replaced others on the billiard tables, women lied to the point of creating in the salons and alcoves a murmur that would drive one mad; nothing certain appeared on the surface of my land. My entire childhood paradise, I found it completely shaven and mute. And at every moment I had to start over the search, not for happiness, but for repose, for a bed, for a quart of pure water, on a terrestrial crust polluted with pustules and cracked with dark consciences.

All this, it's my secret geography. All this, it's my hidden dream, the money concealed under the straw mattresses, the fugitives that we are afraid to admit, and the patience of a sentinel that makes it

possible to wait one day, and then another day, then
weeks and years. These walks between leaves and
stars put me in touch with all-out militarists, slaves,
prostitutes, the dust of women of the world, with
orthopedists, psychologists, tough bourgeois, mush-
room lovers and conquerors. And so, in the long run,
an immense spirit of destruction came to the crown
of my head. I would like to be, out of kindness, the
divine and withered épicier of this continental do-
cility, the butcher of Verdun, the Genghis Khan of
hotels, the Lame Devil, the Gil Blas of Santillane, the
Head of Tears and the Feet of a Skylark. Clouds of
emerald and dew over which hover the messengers
of renewal, sometimes piercing the Mallarméan cross
behind which my bronchial tubes secrete acidic blood.
My memory makes its spiderweb along walls oozing
with moral fat. I'm afraid to walk still farther on the
king's pavement, I'm afraid to my hands, I'm afraid
to my eyes.

And not a murmur of tenderness in this escape
from worlds, no serenade in this volcanism. All these
rivers of conformism, of vagabondage, all these ro-
tations of weeks, of taxis, these strolling excursions,
these fashions, these forms, these weeklies, these
terraces where the same posteriors crush the same
benches, so many fireplaces, with outstretched arms,
of useless efforts, all these oars and seasons, all these
years that ascend along your back like the column

of mercury in a thermometer, a thousand thoughts and a thousand movements toward other dawns, a tailspin of work in the arrondissements of Paris, showers of insects, tidal waves on the boulevards, all for nothing …

I built my world. I have amassed the *steorra* of my universe to see it crumble at my feet in a geography of silt where everything is mingled, the eyes of men and the shape of rivers. None of my harness held together. At the last moment, I may have missed this épicier, … this épicier's wife, this great linchpin that would have withstood transport and misfortune in its case. And all that's left for me to do is to live on rubble, and wander through a burnt-out Capital where I see myself as a ghost.

Walk

I had dinner with an old buddy, far away, in a country of kites and of sidewalks slippery as moraines. And I came back, pushed by a little horned day that seemed to make the earth turn. Under a thin sheet of night, the city lay flattened, like a decalcomania about to be revealed. I went foraging right and left, murmuring my steps, feeling the neighborhoods with a hand accustomed to digging in pitch. Sometimes, I recognized a few corners. I was mentally replacing a bypassed piece in the puzzle. Crossroads, with the smell of filings and of tramways and post offices, the river with a heavy heart under the bridge, the agents, like petrified fountains, like ebony keels in empty squares... I inhaled in great puffs the funereal bird of paradise of the locomotives through the railings, and I thought of those who leave, who wait for the whistle, the hour, the first calf-stroke of the connecting rods, to escape and to flee. But to flee from Paris, what courage. To flee from this city, where all the journeys seem to start from newsstands or buildings.

A long glissade of wind along the dunes of the atmosphere made shudder every cluster of houses with people in them. Low shadows collided. A girl came out of a corner and strode toward another with a bat's side step. The hour weighed heavily, pressing hard, as if to bring centuries of relief underground. And I started walking again in an odor of stalks, so well matched with the red and blue rumors of the suburb festooned with the palmated hands of the plane trees. Was someone calling me? Who? No? No! It was only the shock of the two cold ears of a Wallace Fountain falling on its ribs. A great pretentious young madam from the Wallace Fountain was leaning against the wall of a hospital on which we read: For Sunday, meal consisting of: 1 box of Concarneau sardines, 1 pâté de campagne, 1 Cadoret flan... And the little day nibbled with beautiful teeth on this vertical feast.

From all sides, the windows looked at me and looked at each other. Regiments of streets passed, silently guided by the iron-gloved finger of a tower or church. Footsteps other than mine run toward houses, lives other than mine buckle under tons of disgust. Toward what point must I throw myself, to leave on this end of the sidewalk, panting, drowned in the midst of my shadow, the anguish? But I never get tired of my story; I don't leave my case, my little case. I see and see again, without satisfying my sadness, faces that I really liked. They appear in every window, day and night, in every recess of Paris. They accumulate before the photographer; they welcome me at the cemetery. They come here, to this place where I myself am lost, from the end of a street, and they station themselves ... There is one there, very close, stretched out like a beggar with a soft beard in the moon, leaning against a tree. Who is he, and what does he want from me? I speak and write for all those who walk like me, bent under the weight of their lives. They will stop like me, they will look back on these paths, on these feelings that are gently enveloped in the night. They will think, they will try to understand and fit their story into the immense and moving game of the patience of earthly life. And perhaps one day, little by little, someone, in the centuries of centuries, will manage to return patiently, by little internal shocks, by infiltrations, by muffled violations, with the tread of a wolf, like a trained hunter who approaches without even making the sound of an imperceptible breath, to go back to the beginning of the gust that threw us to the earth, to timidly but finally touch the foam of the immense cataract of the departure ...

Let him hurry, however, this counter-man, this new god, who will start from abundance and gradually impoverish himself in science, alphabets, numbers, sensations, murmurs. Let him hurry, if we run with great strides toward nothingness. The planet razed, would there remain nothing of these corners of feeling? Can only the void remain? The void. This deadly sadness, this silence that is sniffled, the storm filling the sky, pumping springs and hills, horizons and plows. The void. The roar of a castrated monster, this eternal thunder, this kind of enormous beast, occupying all conceivable space, turning and continuously turning again in its sleep ...

So, beyond the seas, the seas, what echo will our unhappy memory seek? "Who will carve my face on the bow of the ship?" said the poet. Because it is always the same music that sounds in my head. I feel it behind my ears, it grows behind my eyes, it drives me to tears. It also rises from the throat, from the chest; it runs through my body like burning venom. It clothes me in solitude. It leads me astray. I thought I was looking for a door, hesitating between two streets, walking in a premeditated direction with a robust and sure step. I only want to emerge from my solitude and put my memories before me.

Nothing makes me take leave of the beloved faces. Here or there, I will continue to live in this room, with the gallops of a piano on a neighboring balcony, or in such and such a neighborhood, in a shower of insects and leaflets, elsewhere again, with absent-minded flashes and parades of clouds, clear or finicky Sundays of boredom, the clacking of carriages, and all their tender almanacs ...

All this life lived, scattered, melted, turning when I turn around, stooping when I bend down, falling asleep when I fall asleep, I see it again often, often, I receive it like a twinge, and I get lost in it, filled with instantaneous hopes that assail me *&* leave me like vertigo. I shall never cease to be stupefied, delighted to have suddenly seen God in the world, as one sees oneself in a mirror at the other end of a room ... And to have seen, clustered around me, five or six smiling shadows that are always my own.

And for a hundred years, I have been looking for these shadows, for a hundred years I have been going through dead ends, knocking on doors, begging for skylights. But the hallways lead me back to the hallways. I'm waiting for my turn to go out. How dark it is, in this world where we end up colliding with our own bodies, seeing ourselves in caravans everywhere! What can I do to avoid these hordes of myself that go up the avenues, stand in line at the stations, occupy café tables? Ah! these twilight streets where, against a zinc-colored sky, a moon, round and bandaged like a wounded head, seems to be sailing, these streets full of doubles that run along the walls, haunting silhouettes, twisted gaits, disheveled figures emerging in a gust of wind under a blow of mocking light ...

Heaven awaits us at every door, at the casement of every street. At every turn, it tracks us down, spreading before us vast expanses of despair, while we trample this earth like a potato that would have fermented one day, in the quaternary epoch, this earth crowded like raisin bread, this earth full of the dead that slipped down, invisible, through a trapdoor. Our bones, an extension of the skeletons of our grandfathers ... The world ... An immense chain of skeletons that hold each other by the hands, by the feet, like a troupe of acrobats that have connected themselves one to another, one to another, who have been deduced from each other, who weave an unnamable hammock that we cannot see which swings above the abyss, and each of which unhooks from the preceding one, falls back onto its feet, receives itself alone, becomes this kind of rocking chair, the easel of Man ...

Now, in this sowing of the city, in this honey-cake where the houses suck in their stomachs, these houses that squint with their human eyes, now, I bend to the right, to the left. I begin this with trodden stone at a young age, this interminable monologue along the towpaths. I walked along these boulevards; I grazed these open doors one after another. Often cold girls, with mouths as blissful as fruits, appeared on the thresholds, hopping, like cuckoos on clocks. Pale and pink girls like the plaster almonds at the baptisms of the poor. They looked as though they were vomited from the cellar and deposited there, like chlorotic chrysalises, invented to agitate the souls of passersby, the loners and drunkards. So, already, I was looking for what I couldn't find. Is this discovery to take place in space, or in time? When will the warning fall from the Unknown? What door will open in the flank of a mêlée of houses? What voice will suddenly call out? Yes, what voice, so that I turn around ...

In the meantime, we have to start looking for the way out, to exit, to destroy more houses, to cross streets as greasy as stoves, to see tramways run along the cobblestones and die, like long perforated spectres. We must see ourselves there, massive, armless, one foot less, carrying three heads, as well as in the distorting mirrors of Luna Park. All these monsters, they are ghosts that I let go, confessions that I made; they are pledges that I gave, so as not to die alone, or too soon. Meanwhile, we must walk, always walk, in this city populated by ourselves. Up there, the grey sky, pensive, inspiring. Further on, the exiled music of wooden horses, of fairground festivals, the muffled beating of drums, the smell of aperitifs, and those distances that draw us farther and farther away ... Tunes hang over the stormy horizon, old sailor tunes. And one can sense, on the outskirts of the city, the clickety-clack of a train, the discontent of a train that we no longer want ... Because the city is full, stuffed, from top to bottom. The city no longer wants trains or men ...

The dawn is torn apart by the sound of sheets. A new day sneaks in that responds to the signaling of the prescribed day. It seems as if someone has shouted: "Next person!" It's a day like any other, flowing with the sound of a sluice, a slow sieve. I get drunk as I listen to it begin under an awning, while men respond to this rebirth with their usual rites. Bakers, postmen, milkmen, salad merchants exit their mole-hills. A café closes. Another, right next door, opens at the same minute, and the owners look at each other, jealous and cross. They will never go hand in hand. Me, I am listening to this day being born, adding one more mystery to those we have yet to unravel, complicating the labyrinth where I stand guard.

First of all, filtering is a bit rushed from time to time, fresh as the sound of a dam, crumpled like a parade of insects under dry leaves. And it's also the sound of weaving, a ferry departure, something like a rain of men that redoubles, a rain that runs, a mucous rain, a heavy rain of plants going to seed, long stems which likely have a brain, a slyly furnished poppy head, and which probably hop on one foot. Suddenly, there's a factory noise, a distant factory noise, a syncopated engine cut by the slapping of transmission belts.

Is this, then, the matter of time? The very sound of the round machine, encircled by grey skies? A great mechanism, which divides the tin footage, the slate paste, the pain of a day, of all these days of life, aligned like the droppings of a palette: a water-hen, a warbler belly, a gutter, occasionally punctuated by the clove of a sharper noise, pricked with a more piercing tone. Bloody days, dead days, elongated, pierced with bullets, and which bleed long, dark nights through their eyes. Murdered days, dead-waters carrying memories, them again, always them, sometimes accompanied by locked voices, voices that float on the surface. I raise my head: it's a far cry from the open-air sounds of the countryside and its cowshed odors, of flint and of honey, of city sounds, of the gymnastic steps around the stone chests where hearts never burn near the earth, but halfway between matter and nothingness, erected, hidden by stairs.

Me, I stand at the edge of distress. I was gently pushed, then thrown out less and less gently, like a wreck, from golden to calm grey, from calm to menacing grey. Today, however, I am standing, more and more solid on my legs, multiplying the world and multiplied by it. It's time to take another step, to move, to carry forward this body already condemned to immobility and which will never find the radiant door. How many days, how many years have I been leaning against this wall? The procession has not stopped: the streets, the streets, always the streets, from here and from elsewhere. Skeletons in their sheaths of flesh, tissue, leather, which pass and pass anew at the step of some parade. Watching them wade through the mud of cities, my body becomes stiff like a statue about to be damaged. All the men of the World are onlookers, watching army corps of streets, the moving prisons of boulevards and squares pass under their windows. And they do not see that they shut themselves up, they do not see that they will never find their way home ...

— It's time, said the ghost.

— Time?

— Yes?

I stepped over the edge of the labyrinth. It was time to open our eyes, to see a bit more clearly. Time also to enter another labyrinth: the quick. I hastily search for my clothes, thrown together pell-mell, I trample them, I am impatient to plunge into another day, to set off again in search ... I am impatient to flee from this black alarm clock, from which I will not get anything, nothing beneficial. We must desert at a gallop.

I begin with the wrong door: I enter the closet instead of rushing to the real door of friends and ushers. My closet is as crowded as Bluebeard's. There is nothing then, nothing, nothing that smiles on the man who knows exactly where he is, who has understood the game well, who recognizes God in all his disguises? I go down to meet the day. And already, I know, I know that I'll go back up later, to close a drawer that I *know* I closed, that I am already closing ...

White Nights

That night, I came home late, tired, slowly, from the thread of my dreams, won over by the day, like a walker surprised by a sea on a lost trail.

I sat in the other armchair, the big Anubis by the window, to listen to him growl a bit and to muster the strength to undress myself. Sleep pulls me back a bit further. One day I will have to put this armchair in order, because it became a silo full of papers, books, letters. It no longer has the form of an ape. I realize that I'm sitting on my briefcase and on the telephone book. Impossible to hold on to it. But I was so tired that I managed to deal with it all as best as I could. Moreover, my underwear had fallen; it had slipped from my legs and squeezed me at the knees in a completely disobliging way. Nevertheless, and while ruminating more and more feebly on the need to heal this discomfort, under the lighted green goblet of the ceiling, I ended up falling asleep.

... Heavy sleep, crossed by dreams of my sick cat, spied on by strange eyes, wet by the noise of a rising tide. I am awakened by the cry of a day that breaks away from its procession and climbs the ladder to my window. The street emerges from the night like a measuring tape, like those papyri that my old friend Comparetti was slowly unrolling with great prudence.

The earth has resumed its walking pace, its trade voices, its grinding stone.

I undress and go to bed, head hot, mind anguished. I can still see once or twice, in half-sleep, my mother, who enters with small steps and offers me my lunch. I send her gently walking, and I descend a bit deeper. … Thereupon the telephone, hidden in my books and in my papers like a cicada, gives three clicks of its elytra. That's it. Too late. The calm has taken its turn in going to bed. And yet I return to sleep, more peacefully, until two o'clock.

Startled awake! I swear to myself that I'll get into it. That I'm in the midst of wasting my day. Must I not now, in the vicinity of Luxembourg, join this noble and doleful young girl, of archaic Greek proportions, and take her to Sainte-Geneviève, where they are devirginizing the room of an Eternal Father bibliophile. There will be, certainly, good people who fart higher than their asses, all the gas light igniters, all the backscratchers, all the official zoophytes, a good many people I know, with ladies, and it is necessary that we show ourselves, poet and poor gentleman, and that we make ourselves believed, and that we give ourselves the importance of succor, on pain of eating a millstone. Besides, I'm not sorry to make my exquisite friend the subject of gossip and whispers that will properly itch the ears of another damn woman who will definitely not fail to poison.

Jumping out of bed. Grooming quickly. My mother cries a bit in my room. We go into the kitchen. She talks to me again about our sick cat. He had come in here with us, she said. Poor mama, we're like that, the rest of us, two old quivering trees.

Now, it's a matter of hurrying, and I splash myself frantically. But what does that mean? (Passage suppressed by the censor. See Aristophanes, Poyard translation.)

Grooming done. Last swipe of the brush to the shoes. A slow, darkly manic inspection of the room and the fireplace, to make sure that I haven't forgotten some little thing, otherwise useless, and that the fragile objects are not too close to the edge of the shelves, risking falling, breaking, and startling my mother.

And, take off! A letter and a card in my mailbox, at the concierge's. A bidding from the porter. Count and Countess of Chamarande. (They almost all make the same mistake. They rarely say: the count, the countess.)

Quiet street. Low mood, the corner of the eye red, a bit heavy. I touch the gate with a tap of my foot, to shut my mouth to the grief that I know will never let me be for one moment. I encounter here, whatever the hour, the gossip and comings and goings of the inhabitants of this barracks, a hospital for the expropriated of a Railway Company. We are in the land of bridges *&* canals. There is a bridge and a guard rail at each turn of these large buildings, letting billow between their jambs a smoke that escalates and blocks the boulevard with a paraph of spectres. And there is always a train sputtering along and suffering or sleeping in its trench. There is the canal, with its overhead gangways cluttered with flâneurs, its scarabs gliding gently on their backs, mandibles in the air, and its roaring sluice armoires. And in the distance, in a niche of green vapor and photographer's rocks, Buttes-Chaumont ...

I like to see all of a sudden, when I turn left, rushing, with my big towel under my arm, I like to frame with a glance this elongated estuary, these confines of la Chapelle, la Villette, and Aubervilliers, crossed by the eyebrow of the open-air railway, under which parading and mumbling squads of funny, idle, and suspicious people, onlookers, sidis, girls who huddle before a wrestler's mat, against a pop-up card game, around a small kid's merry-go-round, whose organ winds and unwinds, till nightfall, a repertoire of three tunes of a barely tolerable sadness ...

Today, everyone seems to be concerned, noises suspended, as if caught in a curious field of silence. And everything that lives floats like smoke, unravels, turns quickly, pivots with a forgetful air, sinks secretly into a door, into the lair of a wine merchant, stoops over, clogs a street corner, melts away, down there, under cloudy days ...

Only, we must hurry. I pass the coiffeur, whose open door reveals three wicked neighborhood gals, seated wisely, palms on their knees, their hair bristling with alligator clips and rollers, waiting for a good two hours. I haven't been to his place since that day when his clerk, before it was noon, had refused me, with a stubborn smile like a sustained note, the last minute razor-blow. And he still had at home, without getting upset, a kind of flunky doorman, in a cap, who didn't make himself useful and who spat out jokes like cigarette butts. It was well worth the trouble of going to lunch the other day, in order to please him, at the little restaurant his mother-in-law owned, and to eat question marks surrounded by an excremental spiral. Still, it's well-placed, that little broth, a stone's throw from the roundabout shaken by engines where direct lines begin, tobacco shops overflowed with smokers, shops with free entry, and where one can see appearing the first tear of the canal...

And coal? I have the time. But how white my charcoal seller is! Beautiful curve, nothing extra. Her bare arms seem to unfold from the source of her ears, through the powerful neck, up to the beautiful hands, like a waterfall of ivory rings. She springs from the counter as from a platform, laughing with all her bells, slyly encircled by the sportsmen of the neighborhood. "But his clock is always ten minutes late." I downed my aperitif in one gulp.

Now it's time to cross quickly to get to the car station on the boulevard. At that crossroads, which is hidden, the moloch trucks and the cars of the big industrialists of Rue de Flandre never slow down, despite the *clous*. The security guard hardly thinks about it. He follows the girls, on the left ...

Taxi. Luxembourg. Naturally, my archaic Greek is gone.

Half-past six. Sainte-Geneviève Library. Ghosts tired at the end of the day. The administrator. The sad, pale associate of an old friend who never spared me. And this little scoundrel, Anthime Choppard, always impertinent, always questioning, and who has never wiped his nose enough! His skull is in a sorry state, his teeth are full of couscous, his voice comes out of his jockstrap. I put him back in his place for the hundredth time.

Return through the claws of my publisher.

On arriving at Rue Château-Gontier, I was given a letter from Grenier, the veterinarian of Rue des Ponts, who, with all sorts of kind words, told me of the death of our cat, my dear Léopion. I'm careful not to tell my mother.

Then, hunger slowly opens its umbrella in the depths of my heart! With a stroke of the cane, I plunge into the breasts of my Aubervilliers charcutière, from where I tear myself away to fall on the spectacles of Bisceglia, the Italian food merchant who recites Dante while unraveling his ham. A pork chop, a heel of Gruyère for me, two peaches for my mother. I eat fiercely, as if I had some thing to kill, I slide into my chair and I fall asleep.

Strange, avid wake-up call at midnight. I leave quietly. Taxi to Brasserie Lipp. A quarter of an hour to Saint-Germain-des-Prés.

... Wittowsky, Lucien de Joyeuse, Epaminondas and his wife, dressed in an atrocious velvet purple evening gown lined with skunks. Marchenoir, whose paper lanterns are decrepit, speaks of a musical ciborium. Dr. Ancelin comments on the role that Desesquelle played during the Commune. Alfange appears at the door, a claw of hair in his eye, tottering like a grizzly bear. Four lights go out. They're closing.

The rest of the night, we spend it as if by chance in Montparnasse, at Poisson d'Or, where the Russian troupe sings, squeals, and dances relentlessly in the little basement with red eyes, where Kalling, to impress two young girls and three comrades, doesn't stop breaking glasses and bottles, which he proudly plunges into his palms, considered from above, from another table, by the centered eye of truth, surrounded with love, of the stiff Mrs. Billaudel...

And then, sleep falling on us like the iron curtain of a closing shop, I return to Rue Scheffer, without

making the slightest noise, into the garden, which
turns blue like the wing of the great Sylvain, I go up
without moving a thing, and, in three clicks, warmed
by a head that no longer wishes to sleep, I settle down
slowly as day breaks with the nightingale which
gargles with the pale must of the sky. And, I note,
absurdly, to cover with ashes this aching heart, this
worried hand, the insect's work of a day...

Horoscope

I know my time. Without having examined with a magnifying glass, a compass, a goniometer, a red light, the point of the ecliptic found on the horizon when I crossed the void with joined feet, I know and recognize myself as if I were a good banknote. When I invite myself to a restaurant in the world or at night, I consent, I let myself go, but deep down, I'm skeptical. I know myself.

My sign is that of the holacanthes, zebra of the sea, Heniochi, barbed ptéroïs, squamous cerniers, spiny fish with suckers and muzzles so blue that they appear close-shaven. I live in the company of seafarers, jazz writers, astronomers, hypnotizers, physiologists, tobacconists, and hoteliers. They are my secret brothers, haunted by the same swarm of maternal stars. All these companions of my time live the same life, drink the same beer, love the same woman, die the same death. I have a number, a day, a birthstone, a climate, favorite dishes, pears for thirst, favorite comings and goings and vices that I do not mix up. I know that I should choose my friends in Cancer or in Scorpio, my mistresses in Virgo, Taurus, or Capricorn. I suspect that everything was foreseen, from the igniter of gas lights who spattered me with old straw every evening when I returned from school, to late arriving trains, and ushers who await me like sentinels at the turn of weeks and years. All the censors, bus ticket inspectors, suddenly broken down taxi drivers, bibliophile concierges are my traveling companions, just as unexpected rain showers, streets that one can't find, banana peels, and sudden hugs, long desired but no longer counted on, are gifts.

I am pregnant, marked, registered, identified. I have a speedometer in my lungs, a scale in my eye, a calendar in my ear, a Michelin map beneath the soles of my feet, mirrors, atlases, key rings, stopwatches all over my body. When I get up, I clock in before starting life, like a good worker. But if I work overtime, no one tells me to clock out. I have twelve thousand senses, wharves of ideas, colonies of feelings, a memory of three million hectares. And I know a lot more.

Like the traveler who paces in the corridor of a train car as it glides into the landscape like a jointer plane, my destiny moves within me, and yet it submits to me. It obeys me. When it runs riot, I restrain it; when it falls asleep, I prod it awake. It believes it is much stronger than me and taunts me, choosing its moment, for example that step between waking and sleeping over which we always stumble. It's then that I generally see it, a bit precious, a bit aristocratic, its eye clouded and cosmic, brain-colored, agitated like a typhoon, restless, worrying, a sort of Gargantua in sailcloth, not quite dreamy, nor entirely threatening, enormous and supple, so immense that it occupies my entire sky, as heavy as sleep, as elusive as a fistful of water, as the presence of a cataract, as an ocean hypocrisy.

And in the morning, when I feel a bit childish, all covered in goose bumps and shivering with indecision, my destiny enters me like a hunger, one of those hunger pangs that suddenly fractures your belly, that works you like a strongbox. I see it and I do not see it: it is part shroud and part migraine, it has a voice that is perhaps mine and perhaps its own, the distant voice of a damaged telephone that gives me grandmother and thug advice, and which I listen to … I swim in it and it swims in me. Pisces.

When I feel that it has settled in me, when we are entwined like those wrestlers to whom everything is allowed and who take advantage of that to return to the navel through the ear, when I descend into it and it descends into me, and when with the round airs of an elastic sphere it guides my affairs, this Fomalhaut begins by lecturing me, and with such high-mindedness that I blunder out of the spirit of contradiction. Fate is a hurricane in a bottle, fermenting in a sternum. A zodiacal sign, the Sign, Yours, the one whose stray bullet you are on earth, is a tidal wave that capsizes you.

Mine is noble. It has a coat of arms in the shape of a fortified boxfish, astonishingly hirsute, bristling with spikes like the Iron Maiden of Cologne. It is the color of an aquarium, full like a country moon, yellow above ponds of blood. It exists more than I do: eternal, well founded, just for all those who have been tangents to it, like a recruiting office. Like those men who have seen once or ten times, who have perhaps even spoken once or ten times, to some milkmaid or Begum, to some cat, to some cousin or sister, and who believed they had rights over her, my fate arrogates rights over me. All my life, therefore, I must have my blood decanted, buy amethysts, write on amethysts, put pieces of amethyst under the feet of rickety tables, and hover in the diaphaneity, and show a predilection for brown? So my book spines will be chestnut, my pupils berry, my socks golden brown, my enemies chocolate, my friends the color of Havana, my mistresses gilded, my maids *café au lait*. I will be the great swarthy native from chestnut boulevards, the brunet guy in the hazelnut pullover who only shows up in the grey hours of the brown and gritty districts to frighten and harm the brûléed whores. And, on top of it all, who will be marooned! All my life?

— All my life, says the Monster.

My uncle had given me a stone for a sledgehammer, an ice-stone, a corundum, a pretty, astringent, and monotone ring that for a long time had served as my comrade. Upon inquiry, it was not my uncle.

That piece of alum, the color of sperm and lettuce, had fallen from the sky to us on a Monday, like an aerolith. No matter how many times we lost it, it found itself again; and when we found it, we lost it again. How many times had I lost my temper against this eye, against this dream debris with its laboratory odor that no sole could reduce to powder, against that kernel of a nebula. Nothing to do, it was fate!

All my life?

— All my life, replied the Southern Hemisphere.

When I go down to the hotel, I try to take room 11. I leave my house at 11 o'clock. I give 11 francs to the ghosts. I bet on 11. I have 11 friends and 11 enemies. I count up to 11.

Finally, it is the 11th hour, before number 11 on 11th street, starting from the Seine, that the 11th chick in a row whispers to me and my 11, taking me for a bonze, in her voice of bronze:

— Hey! said the beautiful blonze. "Come and I'll make you the apoplectic albinonze ..."

A hundred times, I've had the desire to be Aries, Cancer, Aquarius. But then, it would be 13, platinum, daffodil, sweet caporal, coq au vin, suburb. Often, after having despaired of being a man, and free, possessing a hand sans lines, a sky sans stars, as useless on the skin of the planet as an air current, a good word, I dreamed of another zodiac. Of a zodiac that would not force me to marry twice, to introduce myself as a radical-emphysematous deputy in the Trois-Sèvres, to clean my clothes with histogenol or to contract laryngitis when passing before the $ax^2 + bx + c$ agency of the Crédit Lyonnais. Quick, more algebra, fewer predictable alopecias, women without predestination and new dreams under dismantling skies! A zodiac that would be a lemon-press, a fascist, a tax collector, a black tulip, a wackadoo, a philharmonic society for sulfurous baths of railway capitalism. Enough of celestial telegrams, military booklets for single men, extra-stellar passports!

Fortunately, I escape this gathering of souls. No matter how many intellectual symptoms are found in my fingerprints, poetry filings on my envelopes, I remain without past or future. I have no hollows anywhere. I want no other shadow on the ground than the one projected by my wounded tenderness. I am not a naked number on a roulette wheel, and I turn as I please, always infinitely available. My destiny, it's the effort of every night toward myself. It's the return to the heart, with slow steps, along cities enslaved to the bureaucracy of mystery ... What does it matter to me to have been born, to have died, to have one hundred years of hair, predispositions for the merchant marines, a measure of the spirit of contradiction, and faithful women in other people's beds? What does it matter to me that I have my place in this world, which I know for having made it? I am one of those who sow fate, who have discovered the cloakroom before venturing into life itself. I arrived completely naked, free of cosmic tattoos. The gentle giant that bothers me when I still feel deboned by sleep is the Universe that I created for myself, which keeps me warm in my dreams. And if I die tomorrow, it will be from an attack of disobedience.

Paris

The first time that I saw, under the sapwood of Paris, that I really saw, like a true damned one, Hell and Heaven in mobs of men and old women, the first time that we looked into each other's eyes, it was, I believe, a night of vague rioting. I was having an aperitif in a genial little bar, not far from Rue de Lancry, in a sort of cul-de-sac as greasy as the bottom of a frying pan, and which snaked with the smirks of a distinguished tributary toward Boulevard Magenta.

I didn't know the dead end, but I knew the neighborhood, its stenches, its cats entangled in carapaces, like insects, its large blackish crepes that the man kneads on the sidewalk with his foot, mixing under his weight carrots, lettuce, corpses, and dark heels of bread. A taxi had sometimes taken me through these sooty trenches. Yet I had never touched anyone's hand there before. So, one uproarious night, I was there.

In the distance, a kind of soft sparkle, barely perceptible and more like a sulk, was born. None of those who weighed their elbows on the zinc bar-top of the café had heard of any anger in the city. And yet, a strange apprehension crept into us. The bent backs, the oozing necks, the bustle of hands and eyelids, the rubbing of feet on the ground, everything made me think of the specific fears, of the eternal attitudes of the populations that live in the shadow of volcanoes. The day before an eruption causes short fevers and bursts of granules to run over their skin. Invisible sarabands gallop at the level of kneeling fields. Mustard columns are diluted in the green sky. Then, at the first gasp of the boiling mountain, the earth retracts, man flees bent in two, flowers break, cattle whirl round.

Nothing like this in the secret marshes of the 10th arrondissement. We know that a fire will not suddenly spring from the chest of Paris, like a torrid rainbow. On our lands digested by the electoral bacillus, the cataclysm itself is reduced to mediocre proportions. Only a few young banking philosophers, a few privileged sons who went thru life bandaged with diplomas, like those traveling in a berth, find in the colics of the capital Kantian flavors and pre-Columbian jolts. That can be read in their difficult journals; it is detailed in the drawing-rooms where we get together, and Madame de Saint-Céromage immediately believes in causes, in malaise; she jumps toward the beardless, sad minister, an Ecole Normalian in his spare time, and applies cupping glasses and leeches, makes him bleed in haste to know what *the right to work* and *two-tier syndicalism* are. And the other goes with his unctuous words, which he scatters to the four corners of the room. Bigots with mouths deprived of margins, slender

Jews, sweetened with the powder of Rachel, nod with their eyes in the shape of stink bombs. Toreadors in tuxedos, mixed up with Zambezi moralists and sheet-metal workers from Greenland let interpreters know that they got it. The study of the Revolution is also part of their snobbism — we talk about it among crocodiles, penguins, icebergs, nuggets, and giant seeds.

No pedants, in the neighborhoods devoid of nurses and crews. Analysis never risks it, not because it would be reluctant to practice it, but because the men there have a certain dignity. What is athletic is athletic, what is red is red. I had gone to see a cousin, an old cousin who was dying in a fifth floor apartment, who stood behind life, like a trademark on the back of a plate. He seemed happy to be leaving, and told me that he had climbed to the top of the stairs just like anyone else. A relative had given us biscuits, had made them enter into our murmurs. Outside, it was raining glaucos dust. We had sorted out common memories. Then I groped my way downward, swimming down a flight of stairs where aquarium moss wrapped itself around the trunks of the banister. The odor of dark gardens, shy cabbages, hidden soles, and itchy children stirred at the bottom of the shadowy mud. Sometimes, polished doors opened, like surprises at my foreign footsteps, and I saw, ranged around normal tables, pious, thrifty, and well-nourished families. No poetic force seemed to be acting upon them. The patriarch was reading, robust and quiet, walking his fork under the appropriate cheek. The mother was on underwear duty. The children all had one limb asleep. For me, it was a grave opening, happy and well-painted. These people went to life as others go to death. Their heroism isn't known. And yet, they are soldiers. The bell ringing of the gasman, the Inspector General of Elections, or the worldly step of the Lady-Who-Comes-for-Good-Works, makes them stand at attention. In this environment, people respect the uniforms of the Republic.

Higher up, single women, the Eugénie Grandets of the bal-musette, the Carthusians of la Cloche, dreamed, their flesh heavy, the stockings giving way, of dashing soldiers from the cinema. These still young old girls are the aristocracy of the place: what they save goes to Permanente, cotton wool, toothpaste. They snub the concierge and sing out of tune, taunting the neighbors with songs heard outside neighborhood limits and that will not hit the street till a bit later.

In that swarm of dramatic naiveties and virtues, God circulated, a black God, but one who remembered having been Santa Claus. The ghosts had lined up in single file along the steps eaten by tides of feet. And God passed, monotonously, pausing for a moment before the closed doors, as if he wanted to breathe some white hope, a few grams of white hope to the sleeping ones, to the poor who waited for the Lord all night long with their mouths open. I went up and down again. But what floors, what latches, what hinges, from the thin, cold hand of my quivering cousin! Tall houses in poor neighborhoods, tall columns of distress, infinite distances to the heavens. I think of the calls that rise every night from these pits, from these basements full of eyelids and hearts surging toward the sky, like rockets. A Sabbath of genuflexions, supplications, geysers of desires and dreams bloom toward Heaven. Then, the bodies of these humans without a cube of air, human rights … What tuberculosis patient, rent like a bow, will put out the lights at night?

I approach the thin doors. The clutter of life reaches me. Here, the maker of children, arming himself with his pale and hooked Thomas Diafoirus feet, impales a poltroon who has long confused pleasure with bronchitis. There, the squeals of kids echo in a large family geology. We squeeze into the narrow dining rooms: the bicycle is in a drawer, with hairpins, a deck of cards, a green sheet from the tax office, and an appointment calendar. A radio set, shaped like a box and mistuned, screeches. Fingers covered with frostbite set up an alarm clock looking like a sick child's head. At the bottom of this piggy bank lies a pair of concierges, a two-sex divinity who adds to his functions, in these neighborhoods, the obligation of playing the part of the police. Statisticians are informed that the blonde on the 5th floor works the brothels on Avenue de Wagram; that the plumber on staircase A, at the end of the courtyard, frequents clubs; that a sad old lady lives quietly behind her windows, doing nothing, receiving no mail; that the old man who played the flute died strangely, screaming, one November night, and that the whole street was at his funeral. Fearsome as trench cannons, the trashcans adorn the edge of the house, slowly being forgotten under the vault, through a faulty hole.

I throw myself into the street, into this beneficent water that dozes between banks with windows. Fresh water from a street in Paris where one mingles with reflections, water purer than in any city in the world, comforting water, a miraculous spring, from which emits a mixture of courage and hope. I enter a shady café. Two young folks drink from the same glass: one in overalls, one in a bodice, laughter. He, the common man from Larousse, a widespread type, without originality, without value: a good mechanic from the village with hard hands and dog white teeth. But her, the Fleur de Marie...

Drinkers on benches were thinking with all their might. Among the poor, pleasure is enjoyed sitting down. Freedom arises like those big flies with their nielléd behinds. On the walls, military images remind the audience of prestige and ceremonies. Whether they are patriotic or unruly, parliamentary or bloody, it doesn't matter. There are some. There are always games. The paintings that sometimes represent the aperitif bottle and sometimes the bunch of French grapes play the role of museum canvases. A poem about the *bat'd'Af'* rose from all that like the strong smell of a soup. A few lively replies went from four to five mouths at a time to appreciate the things of the day, the sport of the moment. We were among clear, well spread out consciences, served without bones. The boss had an eye to sharing his sausage with the first comer. Choirs of tiny insects sheared through the glasswork gardens. The charm of cheap living spread, emitted with smiles, glares, blows of the tongue and jets of saliva.

I had the feeling that I was in a tent pitched by nomads, in a tent that a sort of hereditary approval of poor devils stretched to the limits of a country, and I saw love, usury, loneliness, conspiracy, debauchery and fury in it. But like a showcase of objects. Barrès, who is often admirable, is amusing, and with him intellectual tourists, who see, beyond certain frontiers, only the prostitutes of external boulevards and the scaffolds of fortifications. Likewise, the population of places sans florists and homeopathic pharmacies see, starting from the Champs-Elysées, only Tyrants & Crœsus. We find in *Du Sang, de la Volupté et de la*

Mort, a beautiful book, but a very refined diary, this surprising note: "Strange, unwelcome young boys, with unexpected and rapid gestures, simulated Father Francis among themselves; poor little sick girls, obscene and nightmarishly elegant, grouped in pairs, in fours, around a bowl of mulled wine." Everything, except the bowl of mulled wine, which is there like a Negro statue at the veterinarian's, everything in this piece, is of a perverse aquarellist. For me, who knows Paris better than the postmen, nothing can look less like an Apache than an Apache, and I absolutely cannot define a streetwalker ... Classes ignore each other, men never see one other, families still live like tribes, with their superstitions, their mythologies, their fears.

I sat close to the couple. The siren laughed like a fruit, and seemed devastated. There is no aristocracy but the youth of women. They are naked in a crowded world. We understand that psychologists and songwriters of cheap sentimentality have made enigmas of them. My neighbor had a laugh that came from the depths of centuries, and a simplicity of gestures that linked her to the Mother of Women. The old men who were there gazed at her with the look of men who let their time pass.

And the man, who was barely the master of his impatient hands, rose by arpeggios toward spheres where his dark dreams sparkled. He felt splendor,

strength, vertigo. He was walking like a Resurrected
Man in a strange ether. He suddenly saw Museum
frescoes flit through his ramified *&* sensitive head.
He came face to face with his double at the summit
of whirling planets. He heard postcard stands tilt
toward his immense ears. He was dying on the
battlefield, distraught, thin and transparent as in
a nightmare, very small *&* endless, and as he saw
himself in the purple stars of drunkenness with his
buddies. A woman is there. One woman, one system,
and so simple, so round! I watched him run across
her and without believing it — because, as the fellow
says, one must be rich in order to have sensations,
— to step over, with a little shame, other existences,
the previous, the future, the imaginary, and the
damned. And the woman modestly, somewhat stu-
pidly, enjoyed these lurches, which they all provoke
without doing it on purpose.

Outside, according to reports, people were getting
angry about oppression. The evening papers passed
through the street like comets. It was said that the
bouillabaisses of the Republican Guards descended
on the slopes of the arrondissements in roller coast-
ers. Tripe sellers, leather workers in their rooms,
girls at the windows, with heavy and cold legs, card
shooters, toothpick bureaucrats, hair-scratchers and
follow-me-young-man madams, Czech vendors, Saar
emigrants, bank clerks, all the creeping vegetation

of the houses of Paris rushed in fragments of bodies
toward the sky, or plunged into streams. All the ideas
of the neighborhood had suddenly been eaten up like
pillows. We had nothing left in our hearts. So, what?
Was the world about to end? Had we found Stavisky?
Would there never again be high literature, poetry,
cinema? In the distance, the famous statues moved
like poplars. All of Paris grimaced. The avenues, the
boulevards, the crossroads, the alleys mobilized their
passersby and their vermin. They poured full buckets
of mirages into the sky. Generals were exploding
like firecrackers. Everything went up. One was lifted
up on his chair, on his wife, on his ideas. The din of
a thousand simultaneous moves ricocheted from
arrondissement to arrondissement. Paris, the city
sung of in all the casinos of the world, Paris, the
city of women, Paris, the city of perfumes, was no
more than an ant-hill bungled by the wooden shoe
of a cowherd. The drinkers and I felt suffocating
epidemics coming upon us. A gentleman-rider was
about to take power. We would drink the blood of the
victims. And then, we would start again, class after
class. The next four would have *sous*, public squares,
well-washed chickens, pedestal tables and marble
objects. We would put up other posters; we would
transform the Vespasians. Religion would become
gymnastic and gymnastics religion, but in such a
brusque and perfect way, the seams would barely be

seen, the scars would be so well-effaced that nobody would be sensitive to the change ...

And then, little by little, the derailment was averted; the curious returned to their shells; the street fell back on its feet. We all found ourselves in the café, stupid, content, proud to see each other in the flesh, friends as before. Alone, the two young people had crossed the equator without noticing it. For them alone, hours had passed. The upheavals hadn't reached them. They were wise and passionate like characters in paintings. They saw everything in white. They climbed unsullied floors, they picked fruit, trampled on ravishing serpents, possessed themselves, twisted in a mirage. They were but cosmic dust: out of space, absent, eternal, and so strange, so comical, so barbaric in that display of glasses, spirits, and mouths ... They lived; we were dead. They galloped in the divine, while we were preoccupied with revolutions. And, in this Paris for a day, I was able to extend my antenna to the marvelous stupidities of two monsters from the Infinite. I have always envied those who prowl beyond the Unknown, who are only eternal combinations ...

... Yet, Paradise was nothing else, before these glacial times when man was dying to carve the stone, when woman was trying to carve out love. Paradise, I hear it above the roof of the city ... And I sense there great landscapes with staggered planes, filled with living things of all kinds, such as have populated Breughel and Bosch. Everywhere, arabesques of women and children around singers and scrubbers, floating lines of knotted hands, flights of caressing eyes. Landings, embankments, medians, half-moons, rotundas, fumivores and carriages loaded with human grapeshot. The stampedes rustle for a long time. Cheerful reptiles of young girls glide into the embroidered countryside. Stairs, steep paths rise under hundred-year-old trees, engraved with names, hearts, and slogans. Train tracks smoke their steam toward the ever-changing identical sky. Steep paths, covered with velvet, lead lovers toward their mirages. Everywhere, gods, dogs, transparent animals jump and dive, make the gravel of fairy tales spring up and shine, heartily kicking their legs, making children stumble, not a cry of which can be heard...

... And then, cheerful or melancholy, confident, isolated in cool courtyards, in gardens, as before as everywhere, as much later as today, in this Paris and in these terrible and treacherous suburbs, in this corner of living-dead men, always lovers, laughing, quarrelsome, united, entwined on doorsteps, imploring, bearing secrets that other paradises have never exhausted, murderers, gentle, so gentle, we others, with the most tender attitudes, dreaming of the arms of the Kanéphoros, of the arms around the neck...

In the Morning

In the awakening of every conscientious man, there is, undoubtedly, an eye that watches him, perched on the cup of café au lait, on the breasts of the egg with ham, or on the Carnelian Dundee. A blond eye like the astonishment of Venus, and clothed in clean water. It's the first censor, the first periscope of this life that begins again, blissful and long, infinitesimal & coriaceous, and which slips away under your feet like a moving walkway.

Take note: it is not from you that the first glance of the morning at the things of the day comes. You, you are little more than an imprint on the winter sports of your sheets. The one who begins life is someone else, and yet it belongs to you, is something that has fallen from you, like a waistcoat button or a ten *sous* piece. I tell you, it is the awakening eye of every conscientious man.

Mine is called Cascaphore, son of the Muses, ball of sleep, a shiny, prim, and gourmet egg, as if he had donned the full attire of Brot mirrors. This eye, it's the monocle hook that I threw out of bed, it's the trap that I set on the carpet, as both my eyes still twirled like rods in the dark metamorphosis. It's the crystal ball of the manufacturers of the future in which the chapters of the day will record themselves, like news items, chronicles, or feuilletons.

Here comes literature and its felt glasses, politics with its acetylene breath, geography with dancing nostrils; political economy, dramatic economy, and domestic economy, the three sisters of love put in the pocket of my dressing gown. Here's the hotel garçon, the love garçon, and the stable garçon. Far away, behind the scenery, I hear the elevator lamenting, built from the reliefs of an old tramway. In a philosophically fresh morning, and with pajamas made of soap-lace, rise the shouts of Saint-Germain-des-Prés, where today I am detained by gas stove matters, an anthill of sciatica, and the butts of unpaid bills. The goatherd sends sausage rolls to the saddler; the Camembert hawker hesitates between *Norma* and the *Musketeers at the Convent*; dogs scratching their permanent refuges perform circus numbers between the legs of the matrons.

All this is the love of living that emerges in the elegance of a star, beneath unkempt roofs. It's my mirrored wardrobe, which casts dying suns into excited fireplaces. It's my sentimental cart-driver soul which wants to absorb everything in a sublime deglutition, even though God had said to it: "Five drops in the morning, twenty at noon, seven million in the evening…"

The horses' hooves play the Ouverture. Richard Wagner wallows on the piano of a concierge's daughter, bought at the Almond Gingerbread Fair.

Mail passes under the door with the prudence of a cockroach. The homeopathic vulture of white nights withdraws and goes to join, deep in the courtyards of Rue Saint-André-des-Arts, the roosters of Bruyère, the shoulder blades of prostitutes, and these ghosts of Paris that are neither Ukrainians, nor Sidis. The Room makes its round of ridiculous legs. The noise of a delivery scooter brings to my ear the exquisite murmur of the streets, as poetic as the tinkling of a kitchen or the purring of old cats, and in which passes the eternal frisson of the absurd: Poulatémen, oh! oh! Kisse Louverti Lallivachna Goloure ... It's the Hindu song of the vagabonds, the Persian poem of the Sexes ...

Gradually, sleep and its seaweed glide over my body of sand and distress, like waves recalled by the bugles of America. I am at low tide, and I can enter barefoot in the correct boats of bourgeois life, dignified and serious. Let's go! One more effort ... The Colonel will enter! I stand at the end of my bed; I am ready. Cascaphore himself has disappeared.

Cascaphore, my nightmare companion, has returned to his faithful doghouse. Tomorrow, to console me for having lived, he will begin barking at the blackthorn. For now, he left me to fend for myself in the middle of a slippery day like a skating rink. Farewell Cascaphore. And to you all, blinds lifted to everyone's lives, hey! What will my first sensations be?

"We calculated," wrote Father Hugo, "that it would take 800 years for a man who read 14 hours a day to read just the works written on History that are found in the Bibliothèque Royale ..." Not a day goes by that that sentence does not return to the roots of my nose, where the very marrow of reflection nests. Eight hundred years, and nothing but History has been unloaded on Rue des Petits-Champs since the stupefying ink of that sentence! To Memoirs, to newspapers, to confidences! Eight hundred years ...

I then go into a trance. All the divine fire of man and the secret ringings that he maintains with Paradise spring out of my indignant sensibility. Thus, am I only the letter F in the Alphabet of Worlds? Am I just a needle hole in the warehouse of Encyclopedias? Misfortune! Misery of life. As I stomp on my hotel carpet, rushing to throw two more sugar cubes into my café au lait, everything happens, in one instant, everything becomes, everything blooms, everything dies. The past, the present, and the future come together in a wedding of pearls. The newspapers, the naked and sweaty women of the world, the suburban accordions, the Council of Ministers, the sea and its turbines exquisite as the loins of young girls, the dizzying seed of the Michelines, the Sorbonne, the Uffizi Museum, the Cordillera of the Andes, the death of Ravel, the microphones of Léon Bérard, Valéry, and Claudel, the voice of Fréderic Lefèvre and the "encore" of the Young Ladies of Cinema, the Province, the turf, the pickpocket, the pot-au-feu, the dry seborrhea of sea-wolves, the souls of others, the sewing, the fear of being kicked by Venus … You and me, them and me, Paris and me, everything and me. It's true, and it's frightening, all of this exists at the same time. And I am doomed to a single life; I am ordered to slide until dawn on only one track. We have but one life, my brothers, one destiny. Each of us is excluded from the hive by some place. And the one who kidnaps the richest of the Peruvian women at night will not discover, on the quays, that map of the sky that Louis Barthou dreamed of … One cannot be both Dante and Shakespeare, the Horse of Auteuil and the Queen of the Meadows at the same time. Yet, the desire to be a whirlwind engulfs me. I cannot accept of myself this reduction in the poetry of government. At the same time I would like to be both with my mistress and my publisher, with the patron and with the clothier, with the friend and with the traitor, in the tramway, in the stratosphere, and under water. I want to build myself with houses and die with parachutes …

My heart screams to be alone in the midst of solitude. Alas! man is the desert of deserts. Fortunately, God, or the mystery that takes its place, has given us Cascaphore, that Phanodorme of Green Nights. Only, in fact, sleep throws us onto the tracks of Eternity and allows us to transform into a lemon-squeezer

the mother-of-pearl navel of some beauty glimpsed at
the Opera ball. The poet is the man who most desires
this ubiquitous storm, this Sudanese grasshopper life.
The life of presence and invasion. The bourgeois is
the one who desires it the least. Only the nightmare,
a kind of plunge into original sin, authorizes it and
permits us to bite into an always-blinding part of it.
Cascaphore is my abstract Asmodeus, my fishing net.
And if I like the bed, it's also that I find myself in it
at the Museum…

Leaning

Leaning on my window, I watch the news, the feelings, the pants, the heads of soldiers and the hearts of spring pass by, heavy eyelids and oranges waxed like cannonballs, all in the sweetish halo of Mr. Bedloë's memories. The panorama unfurls, like a sheet of decalcomania between the fingers of a child. Shadows of students, workers, and hunted lovers tangle in a gun-club bouquet. And from the top of my balustrade, I see the vans of the market gardeners, the buses, cars, and taxis that compete and consider each other ready to have it out for the great cataclysm of the streets, while the demons of the sewers rise, adorning the bitumen and fabric landscape with movements of pride and the humor of Naja tripudians.

Anxious and pallid passersby look for doors, like the five daughters of Orlamonde. Long lines of faces and backs come and go on the belly of this nursery. The trees of the 6th arrondissement and the sidewalk loves, wheels with worn lips, hollow-toothed shoes, and some alopeciac intellectuals accompany the procession up to the point of Saint-Germain-des-Prés to descend anew toward the rails of the Gare de Lyon. My eye plunges into the fate of these wide-awake night owls.

Leaning on my window, I suddenly feel myself drawn to these abandoned skulls, these poor skulls of the École Maternelle. And I would cry long hours of tears over these silhouettes that take my place in the crowd — yes, I would cry with impatience and fervor, I would cry out of loneliness, if I did not know that I too, just now, I will let myself slide on the discolored and bruised stone, my soul deep in my pockets, my pockets gaping, my life as heavy as a wet newspaper and my eyes tired from nights of memories.

Already, the restaurant is carrying out its loving work, the manager of the Hunting Horn brushes his frock coats as delicate as the lives of insects, the dairyman decants his ripolins, the pipe dealer cleans his cerebellum with a brush glistening with nicotine. Great noises of meditation mixed with enthusiasm, rapacious anger, violence against others, combinations of hearts, the hum of ambition, all flourish in an invisible earth and rise in fresh sheaves to the point of my despair. I am the man of the steamer who is driven by dark desire to throw himself into that water of men and of females, to drown there my hatred of constraints and my weariness of listening at the gates of life.

Leaning on my window, I see the taxi and its shadow the fiacre, the passerby and his neighbor the corpse, the eyes that lie, the employees that believe themselves to be popular men, the women

who engird the bored rich and the love that rots at
the edge of their mouths. My gaze descends to the
humus of this tingling. I am moved by so many destinies that trot like sarigues between two boulevards,
between two meals, between two worlds, Raspail and
Saint-Michel, the bit on my feet and the ruse on my
nails. Formerly, a long, fat, secret thing where the
pillagers and the carriages sneaked in, where they
suddenly perceived, like a star, the furtive foot of a
princess, the eye of a hardened soldier, or the rosa-
cea of a devotee, the streets consoled, no doubt by
their mystery alone, the wreckage of the passerby, or
frightened or killed him. There is, in the past of sidewalks and doors, a whole side of Alexandre Dumas
whose meticulous fantasy has always got me by the
guts. Today, it is only the military movements of the
Parisians, uniform and intertwined like clover sprigs.
The same overcoat covers a thousand shoulders; the
same omnibus serves as an armchair to a thousand
larvae and carries a greenish snout swollen with
the hurly-burly exiting from a factory. At daybreak,
the 15 tons of vendables, regular as rapids, enter the
station, brakes straining and tires raging. The ears
of the chimneys of Rue du Four curl up like acacia
leaves, the eyelids of the bakeries jump, the robust
and sad drunks pirouette on the heel of a skater and
cling to trash cans.

But, from my window, when this artillery burst the city like a bladder, I can still see shadows twirling. Diaphanous and slender, the ankles of sirens circle round street lamps. The moon of Paris penetrates the benches, the drapes, the iron curtains, the mops, the earthenware, the soap, the wallet folded like a sex organ, the sex organ that has the value of a wallet, and this heavy, mauve liquid that flows in the eye as we close it under the pressure of sleep.

Oftentimes, I am exhausted from attentiveness and patience. There seems to be a burden on my shoulders that will keep me from getting up. My arms will enter for eternity into the wrought iron of the abutment, and I will always watch, like a tree, entirely alone, like a lighthouse, the ant-like movements of the men whom I touch with a long gaze. Often, interruptions are formed in my bent pose, and I feel behind my back that life is calling me: it is the telephone and its lasso of dialogues, its words flinging themselves at you like parents; it's the postman and his orchestra of stamps, his card games, his toy carpenter's kit from Galeries Lafayette. It's the person one doesn't expect, and who, we think with cold sweats in the ears, risks blocking the way of the person one does expect ...

So, the chore is done. I rush toward my windows again. And, when it is too late, I imagine them, lying down, I fall asleep on the back of a dream, like a despairing Mallarméan. My curtains draw into my congested room all the roofs of the street and its windows and its shops. Life is there, in the dreamy, buzzing smoke. It's the cracking open of a better world than that which I imagine, with a warm neck and a ruminating heart. I can imagine, behind the cement, the cut stone or the brick, solid frames of egoism and consideration. I can imagine, behind the serge, the comb, or the cheviot, meager resistances to temptation: tobacco, an aperitif, the tramp, the crime-filled suburban train…

Leaning on my window, I feel my life trickling drop by drop into everyone's cemetery. I see my desires follow a procession of the poor to the mass grave where thistles, stones, and keen-eyed critters await me. I am no longer a man of memory. The mistresses of old no longer inhabit my shriveled heart. They left little more than debris. Neither art nor politics, hunger nor ambition, would make me change my place now. I love this vespasienne draped in its crinoline, this carriage with the beautiful buttocks of male asparagus, this tram that returns from Châtelet, quite surprised to no longer find its tracks. I love that man who walks away, all alone against himself, brushing against the walls; and I love this woman, harried and not very elegant, but cheerful and fragrant like a basket of fruit. I see her, short and violent under her mantilla, slipping like a color on a palette, darting through the crowd, like a quick laugh. She passes by, she does not raise her head: her senses are still not sharp enough to hear my call.

Leaning on my window, I see that the world is nothing but a game of skull bowling. And I soon see nothing but hats, nothing but hats, bowlers, fedoras, caps, all the dark and shaggy hardware of women, and always hats. And under the hats are the hairy scalps, and under those scalps coated with the spirit of contradiction are ideas ... Some slip through to me in the signatures of climbing plants; others descend toward the mesentery of the idler, like the roots of a black radish. The emotions are more perceptible and more vivid. Hatred, always the first to bear leaves and fruits, wanders and fumes. Its smell soon leapt to the nostrils of the watchman. Here is the desire, the friendship, the confidence, the sense of happiness, the lust for laziness, the disposition to jealousy. A sort of broth is being made before my eyes, in this crossroads, where everything is simmering together: rowboats and gaiter buttons, the old and the new; the intelligence of Mr. Ipartakofu, an austere and snobbish Jew, and the delicacy of Mrs. Thusdie, born Lamouru; the tact of my friends Craven, gunsmith, Hoof, sheet-metal worker, Imbroglious, genealogist, and the Count des Shutmouth, arbiter of elegance.

Yes, my soul, all that you see, it's life, all that you examine with a sigh, it's life. Let's remain, the two of us, a hundred years and more, let's stay with our arms on the balustrade, our bodies leaning against the railing, prudence sharpened, let's remain and resign ourselves. Let us not descend into this threnody; let's not be confused by the noise of false souls, of hearts eaten by worms, of poisonous spirits. Yes, let's stay together, you in the middle of me, me around you, you suffering, me struggling. Let us sometimes close our eyes, try to put between the street and ourselves, between ourselves and others, oceans of mute lyricism, ramparts stuffed with hydrophilic cotton. Let us return slowly to the memories of skipping school, both of us whispering with a wolf's step to images gleaned from long adolescence. My soul, we were rolled into the dust of false oaths, we were promised not only rewards that we did not want, but kindnesses, "myosotis of love." We were led to believe that we were smiling, that we were loved, that the hands that slipped into our hands were clean and free of thorns. O slip of disappointments & tortures! For us there were never any righteous effusions, or sincere palms. They even wanted to separate us, and to break you deep inside me, my soul, like an elixir in a shell.

I saw the mouths that I loved lying; I saw shut, like drawbridges, the hearts in which my confidence was shutting like drawbridges; I have surprised hands in my pockets, gazes in my inner life; I heard whisperings on lips that had only accustomed me to cries of affection. They formed fasces behind my back, they declared war on me, they robbed me of smiles, handshakes, promises. Nothing, nothing was left to us, my soul. We only have the street before our eyes and the cemetery below our feet. We know our desperate hymen is being joked about. We hear that people are coming with scythes of blood and gall to cut the last grass from under our feet in order to better show us the path to the grave.

But we shall be strong, my soul. I will be the bolt and you the nut, and we will be able, for a thousand and a thousand years, to approach the waves; we can lean on that window of distress. And then, in the murmur of our waiting, one pathic evening, some creature will come. We will recognize it by its clandestine purity; we shall guess at its fresh words. It will come to close our eyes, to cross our arms over our chests. It will say that our love, all this love that we have not seen, all this love that we have trampled on, that we have bruised, yes, that our love is no more than our eternity.

So, my soul, while I am lying there and already rustling, you will go and lean on the window, you will put on the beautiful clothes of the sentinel, and you will cry, you will cry with all your might!

We will hear.
Who is this We?
Who? you ask?
But every soul knows.

Erythema of the Devil

At the fuliginous hour when the hearse itself blends with the ghosts of the tunnels, when the naked women of the cabarets of Paris make their way toward paid vacations or the bourgeois curtains of the bedroom fill with hiccups from the enigmatic husband; when the socialites finally committed suicide according to the forecasts of their book of hours; when the hallucinating turnip makes, by the smoking, grumbling Arpajonnais, its entry into the Capitol at the head of the nocturnal parade of vegetables; when there is nothing left of the dry, drained, cast-off day but the feathers of drunkards and the shrapnel of cigarette butts on benches, sometimes also some distant rattle of a typewriter, some poet without bed or legs, some backside beatified on the paradise of buried fortifications, then, the Devil ascends.

Prince of Invertebrates, eternal and obscene campanile, undertaker of the Astrolabe, I see him appear and grimace, this aggregate, this encaustic monster, polished at the corners, supple as a trapeze artist; I see him hopping at the far end of night, this varnished Moor with twelve leather navels, with damascened gums, galloping from moon to moon, like the white-toothed Corgète of those half-Persian, half-macabre tales, which no one wrote nor will write.

He approaches the ramp that separates the mortal public from the supra-normal stage and greets, as his knees spring up like beech twigs and crack under the weight of his invisible and traditional irony. And entirely drunk I can then contemplate face to face that illustrious, uniformed rooster from the nightmares of my first communion, the perfect intruder, the formidable and rubescent reincarnated one, the hooked, the hanged, the nutwhoellah, the mygale man with a laugh like a goat, as well as a door-lock. I see him slip through the harsh night and wallow on the whites of the eyes of sleeping men. I see him take possession of enclosed brains and the secrets of the sexes, this giant lampyris with mermaid teeth. I see him rock, cuntspire, fornicate, thunbed and coglutinate, this epic and sly devil, a bit Jewish, a bit melancholic, dignified and funereal, susceptible, entirely juiced-up with leaps and pranks, a crusty and solid hermit who sprinkles us with a geyser of laughter, a water game of esoteric marmalade, where we begin to step lively with our webbed feet and the varicocele of our meninges.

The Devil is the real One. He's the Mummy of Great Caliber, a living mirrored armoire the World has dragged after it since it was a world, like a dog dragging around, attached to its tail, the children's casserole dish to Poulbot. The first time that I heard, still very young, these two verses, sipped by some poet from the Chat Noir:

I put the surplus of my too much
In the nevertheless of your worst ...

I understood that the Devil was not far away, and that he was going to give me a troubadic tripping, a sound rap on my toes in a cozy corner of Boulevard de Clichy. It didn't happen until eight days later. The Devil took the form of a gasman and, while our servant was cleaning, the demon showed me his hunting satchel, made of minister's skin, wherein the eternal ashes of his portable Hell were accumulating.

We falsely believe that the Devil has disappeared from our political regions and has been entirely repainted with anti-clerical and impermeable sentimentality. We believe that he has evaporated, like some species of relatively uncommon fish. With the help of a few schoolteachers eager to step over everything that separates them from the talking bibliophile and unlimited caviar, supported by the magazines for today's women, now sporting, metaphysical, right-handed or left-handed up to the sluice, we believed that the world had clarified itself, that it had become as simple as the head of a shaved soldier, as sympathetic as the literature of Coppée, of Theuriet, of certain living persons whose names we shall withhold, as palpable as fabric, as edible as an apple; in short, that the world had no more underside, depth, mystery, or inexplicable vertebrae than cinematographic film. We were mistaken.

Scarcely have I opened my eyes in my district than
the transmitting station of my neighbor sprinkles me
with a T.S.F. pizzicato, where I sniff the Devil at once.
I lend an ear: DE DE V V IL IL ... murmurs the
drop of tap water that falls like the sound of an insect
into the semolina of the sink. He's there. He no longer
has for us that Mephistophelian vocabulary that once
betrayed him to desperate and twisted imaginations.
He is no longer medieval; indisputably, he is clothed
in the tuxedo of our realistic anxieties. He appears
without pomp in the marrow of our moments. And,
so long as we waste time in thinking about him, in
speaking out against his presence, he calls us to order
by some smoke, by some abjured image of his former
luxury. Barely have I spoken, for example, when the
cold-water tap starts to hiss louder than the other,
while the garden layout of the central heating system
pants as if it were breathless before a hundred meter
stretch. A cascade of rubble and nervous scrap metal
suddenly pierces the water of the street! I get up to
run to the window. It's Moloch, the hippopotamus
of Les Halles, who is stationed with his wardrobe of
quarters of beef. His heavy nostrils of black butter
and poppy meat transpierce the dawn, supported
only by the gymnastics made fashionable by the athe-
istic ministers of the Third Republic, and some old
adjutants who will be appointed prefects before the
ambassadors barely give them space. And the Devil

unscrews himself from the radiator cap to invite me to contemplate the devastation that our human heads have spread, like bad pâté, on the virgin bread of the planet.

The turd of Jupiter shines like a new coin in the middle of the chalky sky. A god with the face of a dead frog, a cigar of God, an atom of God, ventures out of this backdrop and sees on the machine, on the earthly carousel, nothing but miserable mushrooms overlapping one another, sad, flat-footed men running after flat, sad chimeras. We lower the storm blind. Convulsive motorcycles whisper the madness of the cities in a language of pedicures and scruples. From the mouths of the sewers to the mouths of love, the swell of men precipitates itself, howling with apprehension, trembling with death, annihilated by daily tension. It doesn't know where it is going, nor why it lives another day, why that day is named February 18, or something close to it. It does not understand why young men cry for women, why women weep for honors and banks, why nothing exists of what we read or sing, when everything exists of what one never says to anyone, of what no one will ever know, neither here, nor far beyond. For we know nothing, not even what a friend thinks of us, not even if that trusting head that sleeps on our shoulders, all slobbered with happiness and imbecility, is not hatching some plan to dynamite us, us and our poor furniture, us and the tender dogs of our private life.

As long as we are afraid of ourselves, as long as the brain has not become something as precise as a kilo of salt, as long as we turn around in our sheets wet with desire and hate, as long as we ask ourselves if we are adored, hated, if it is good to live, if it is better to die, if we will win wars or matches, as long as we encumber ourselves with the unexpected, with chance, with destiny or providence, there will be some Devil in the air.

We can have a calm imagination. Someone watches over the fantastic and can hear themselves fiddling with the curves of our grey matter. Suddenly become a useless functionary since *Gaspard de la Nuit*, Satan, whom official science and the S.F.I.O. party believed well dead and buried, Satan, who was medieval, romantic, Baudelairean, Rimbaudian, Verlainean, Clemencist, Bergsonian at times, anarchist, and even, let's say it, Gidean, terrorist, Barrésian, Spanish, Montparnassian and bourgeois, Satan, become *Satant*, projection of a radical-socialist myth, officer of Territorial and Public Instruction, Satan has never dreamed of leaving this comfortable land of prebendaries where he is not too bad off, and on which nobody has ever seriously put in question his practices.

And besides, where would he go? It isn't easy to imagine in our days this demoniacal move, and the profaners themselves would be hard pressed to assign to Mephistopheles a domicile less fantastic than that of men.

Suppose that we catapult him toward some infinity? The Devil would quickly storm into our spiritual democracies. The Devil is a tomahawk, a boomerang that bears our trademark and lives off the blood of our children's children. Besides, where would he lodge his thickened, bifid tongue, laden with scoria, his raven beak become babine, his pitchfork become fish knife? Would he like to retire, resign, ask for a tobacco shop, the position of administrator of the Théâtre Français; the one who would rather follow his own path, Secretary-General of the Syndicate of the Patrons of Lupanars? Or to flee, betray men, drown women, cross the frontier of frontiers, that imperceptible dotted line which separates that which is from that which is no longer? No. Whatever he does, we would immediately go out of our way to hold him back by the velvety braids of his quivering tailcoat, all covered with goose bumps.

I see that carnal descriptions of the character are scarcely ever made, and the theaters themselves are reluctant to horn the actor like the Devil. Only, perhaps, the stages of Nevers or Barbezieux, if they wished, could throw themselves into a pantomime worthy of the name. But, from one end of the map to the other, the world today is too reasonable and too large to believe that the demon has a form, a shadow, attributes and accessories such as horns, tongue, tail, pointed shoes, oxyhydrogen blowtorches, snakes in the pharynx, flashlights, shrieking beasts in a sling bag, return tickets to Hell, intentions in the form of cobblestones and monkey money. It was only the secondary romantics of the epoch of Louis-Philippe who would clothe him and do his hair, shine his shoes, starch him, emboss him, offer him a chair, pamper him as if he were a tenor of the Opera, a champion of wrestling, a financial inspector, or a minister finally suitable for governmental matters.

Nowadays, and especially since cosmetic surgery, television, bathroom and migraine music, since the Flan Popurel and the intellectual circus, the smallest boy-scout, the most naive of bellhops, well know that the Devil is a feeling. But a general feeling, not an individual one. A feeling of assembly, of nation, of public square and of federation. Something like an opinion to the hundredth power, the steamroller of the fine weather of the war in lace, the obsidional fever, the storm, the simoom, the opening of the hunt. A feeling that is visible, that vomits into corners like ectoplasm. I showed the Devil to my charcoal seller, who — I remarked to him — was ill prepared for this apparition, although it was normally contained in his sacks of black petroleum. The good man laughed, shrugging his shoulders as mirth rolled in the air. A few allusions got the better of him.

— What if I could, I said to him, prove that not only did I pay you, but that you owe me money? What if, while you are guffawing in a fumigation of dust, your wife had a perm made by sharp hands and always lower than her hair? What if the telephone call announcing a big order came through your shop while you were right here? What if your horse suddenly felt itself grow wings and begin to deliver your head to the sparrows hovering over the rooftops like a reverse Santa Claus? What if this charcoal cascading into my cellar carried diamonds as large as the more elegant ones? You want me to give you a hundred francs, my good man? But, search your pocket well — I just gave them to you! Hold on, here are the intestines of your ancestors mingling with anthracite and which you have the gall to sell by the kilo, instead of savoring them yourself with your own! And finally, you will come out of here all oozing with satisfaction, your duty done, the coal poleaxed like the dregs of Chinese ink. And, in the street, right in the middle of the pavement, you'll find yourself face to face with a competitor who is about to knock you out, a truck driver who will mow down your wife at the corner. How can you laugh, while these possibilities are waiting for you and aim for you night and day?

The charcoal seller ran off to see, not the evil foundation of my words, but the chances of the Improbable. For it is enough to lend an ear to the

murmur of the almanacs and to simply listen to
the drip of the liquid of the years that we squeeze
from our dripping souls: those are only anonymous
messages and macabre cables, which the postman
distributes to us, joyous undertaker, and his printed
matter: Communication from the Beyond; astrologers'
banks, witches' toasts, worldly or clandestine cabals
with police prefects in sleeveless vests, enchanting
police, adjustable horoscopes through treaties with
rewards in kind, chicory or sponge-napkins, news
items evoking Mélusine or Circé, chit-chatting graves,
acrobatics of the zodiacal ring, Berthelot's views of
the chemical era, apparitions of American sylphs,
from Yugoslav dwarfs to the mathematical sky, per-
fecting interstitial Voronovian grafts, explanations
of nightmares by crossword puzzle professors, type-
writers in hand, magnifying glasses for sensitive feet,
skeleton mustaches, parades of playing cards, coffee
grounds served at home by troops of fakirs formed
into secret societies, Supernatural hymns, intuitive
airplanes, dowsers of clogged brains, Pythias of wash-
basins, all of which constitute the Sambre-et-Meuse
of the Apocalypse.

The Devil, who had become a hermit, changed his
profession and preferred that of poet for large-cir-
culation newspapers. We no longer wanted to admit

him to the biblical past; it will be necessary to situate him in the Unforeseeable. It is he who prompts us to know what will be contained in the coming year, the day at hand, or the imminent hour. Solicited by politicians, archivists, surgeons, bankers, actors, and merchants, a magician from my neighborhood, leaving Canal Saint-Martin the way the Truth comes out of its well, told me that she was reduced, by these times of uncertainty and hot impatience, to read not for the future, but for the evening, for the pocket, and for the pink of the gums...

In short, the moment no longer suits us. The Devil makes us itch to understand and calls on us to know what the other moment will contain, the one that we have just begun. I am told today that these elements of a new fauna, some reactionaries, of the right or the left, it doesn't matter, do not return home without consulting the witch. Precaution of the possessed. You never know: the evil eye can descend the stairs four at a time, weeping its malefic sperm, as you innocently prepare to put your unbeliever's foot on the steps. An unforeseen guest may have been invited without your knowledge by your stupid wife, or present himself, as you are in the midst of putting on your pajamas, present himself as terrible and courteous, as described by Henri de Regnier, who claimed to me to have seen the Devil often, and even with the most classic of companions.

All in all, each one of us today is tortured by the last word. The last word, or the "Great Mystery." Reading the last pages of European or Martian newspapers, American or Asian periodicals, Black woods and positivist sheets will justly seize the attention of rationalists and the devils of another century, when we move on to the rejuvenation of cadres. For never before, since the Chaldeans, has the art of predicting unfolded with so much luxury and ingenuity. Never had the Devil allowed such an Olympic record to sink into our miserable skulls all sticky with saltpeter. Send a handful of your hair, torn out with your left hand on a Friday morning between 7 and 8 o'clock, to such a thaumaturge, and you will more surely win at the National Lottery than you will catch the flu. Give your date of birth on "velvet model" powder-paper to a Hindu, this man will tell you your future, and you are sure to marry richly. Have you a property near Paris? In rainy weather, call on a member of the Ku-Klux-Klan, armed with a conductor's baton, to come in on tiptoe: he will be in charge of detecting the casket of the Golden Scarabee, the charcoal, the platinum, the Hungarian sausage, caviar, the Maritime Perlimpimpin, golden mud from the Invincible Armada, spaghetti and Roquefort, in the honey arcana of your suburban land.

This mysticism of the Unknown made amazing progress in the Twentieth Century, that of the electric devils. There isn't one of these ladies, in society, in conferences, on the carpet or in the kitchen, who doesn't "consult" him at least once a week. The devil understood the times perfectly. He joined the ranks of hairdressers, manicurists, lovers and masseurs. Soon, magic and diabolical invasion will replace the cinema, adultery, slander, the re-stitching of silk stockings, sporting lust and the pleasure of bank accounts. Reasonable and level-headed citizens, who cannot help but grumble about the passage of the monarchist, the communist, or the government employee, play cup-and-ball with their hats as they see the necromancer, the alchemist, or the Sybil of foam, as said Alphonse Allais.

Professions honored today. No human being currently inspires as much respect as the one who splutters in your hand, who dips his feet in coffee grounds, ink stains, molten lead, crème fraîche; who auscultates the end of the cigarette, the fingerprint, the serous fluid, the relief or the arabesque of sweat that your underarms draw in the depths of your overcoats. He goes farther, because the devil is armed with strong magnets. A friend of mine, serious down to the shining of his boots, recommended to me in these terms a doctor from his circles: "You know he's a bit of a wizard!" and to run forthwith to the ghost! We no longer even want professions to be pure — we need the devil!

And the Devil goes everywhere, slips into the simplest enterprises. We don't want to believe in him anymore? We drove him out of our attics, out of literature, the arts, we sprayed his cobwebs with fly-tox, we pumped the demon into puddles of love and emptied the potions? Good. And now the Devil takes revenge by whispering to us that Friday will not be like Thursday. He lets us know that we can change our destiny if we give ourselves a little effort, that the powerless will have big hits tomorrow, that glory, ardor, health are scarcely worth a piece of bread. The Devil became anxious and profited from our cowardice. He plays on our cowardice. He speculates on our weakness. He circumvents and enchains us, splashing us with blinding elixirs.

In my solitary den, where the furniture stiffens upon my arrival, and nudges my elbow by imitating the cry of a goose as soon as I have turned my back, I find the prince of salsify installed on the organs of the central heating system, the mesentery in the sun, and the laughter ringing around his Onanistic owl head. There he is, like Dostoevsky's demon, playing cards. My presence does not push him to the confines of the perceptible. He taunts me with his titles and fills me with affectionate distresses. O Diable d'Hôtel, Emperor of Sycamore and white wine Polyhedron, viscera with eight uses, like a Swiss Army knife, a stepladder, the ink of a pen and the committee-hungry opportunist! His life rests, like so many French lives, on the current quadruple hitch: modern comfort, political camp, vegetarianism, controlled sexuality. There is no devil less visible than that spot of shadow on the wall. I can calmly descend into the bourgeois bath of my dump filled with palpable and ridiculous accessories. Light! Strength of soul! Help! My nerves shoot with the bow, against this felt ventriloquist, this abstract Devil who intoxicates us like aspirin. My collar button vaults over my skull, all waxed with common sense, and I jump after it, and I see three million faux collar buttons, a vitrine, a whole copper factory galloping in the dust blue corners. My hands tear along the disjointed slats. And the buttons take their place next to the ribs, while the Devil opposes my little way of life, and retards the clocks with a robust laugh that reminds me of so many things...

Advocacy of Disorder

I fear Order, as conceived by the pawns of the ill-understood spirit of rigor, — which have not ceased to irritate me, — as I fear the too blue sky, the too calm sea, and love without disputes. Order is a flying trapeze number. Let a butterfly pass before your eyes, and there it is, the threatened number! Their order is as rigid as a fake collar, taut as the nervous system of a tennis racket. It's the wire that burns the soles of the dancer's feet. It's an instant of perfection that terrifies the mind like the idea of the highest speck of snow from Mont Blanc! It's the frozen point of the thermometer that will die. It is also blind obedience and terror...

I dreamed of order in the form of a new deck of cards: it signified nothing. It was pure as a newborn's brain. Order is a closed orange, the sleep of a virgin, the silence of the deep, the useless heart. Ordered pockets are empty pockets. A house in order is a house where, in a large living room, you can see ghosts sitting in a circle chatting about morality; it is a kitchen without activity and without smells. Order is a network of railways: trains of ideas, trains of feelings, trains of inclinations always circulating at the same times, precise, buttered with conventional elegance.

When my room is in order, I leave it. When my loves are in order, I turn away from them. Order, it's a dentist's waiting room, a dusted room, sadly coquettish, impersonal, and silent, and you suddenly realize you're no longer in pain. And you would remain there, useless, indefinitely... You'd be one of the links of order. You'd take your place in the correct and ordained time...

To a large extent, order prohibits smoking, forests, journeys. To desire order in a systematic way is to desire the clinic, the duty of vacations, the uniform, and death. For the most beautiful order is the Order of Death. There is order only in alphabets, grammatical rules, memories, and cemeteries. Order is *under* the waves, *under* the grasses, *under* the passions. It is in the past, in what is no longer disturbing, in what will never move. Order, it's the saints of the calendar, seasons, natural boundaries. But what would such order be without the madness of men? Quite simply it is a nest devoid of birds, a park devoid of children, a hand devoid of lines.

Order, it's Buddha, it's Mohammed. It's a great king, and these are the names of the characters in his court: Symmetry, Classification, Method, Subdivision, Ensemble, System, Alignment, etc. Yet, I put nothing in line...

Take note, however. Disorder is not the opposite of order. Just as order is not an arrangement, disorder is not a derangement. Disorder, it is neither the storm, nor the vibration of windows shaken by passing vehicles, nor the inverted head, nor the plow before the oxen. It's life itself. Order presupposes *the appearance* of disciplines, of immobilities, of tombs, of laws, of structures, and it only gives birth to iconoclasts. Because the fatality of order is the invitation to stampede, to insult, to rifts, and to thawing. Order is a static God. Whereas disorder, as real souls understand it, is man in motion.

Order permits nothing. It ends the racing of impressions and of currents like a bulwark. It's the station where we arrive. On the other hand, disorder is the station from which we depart. Order is called terminus and disorder is called escape. Order is the multiplication table. Disorder, it's Victor Hugo. War is the domain of order, because it tends toward an end, toward limitations, it presupposes hierarchies, organizations, groups. But one fine summer day, on the banks of the Marne, elbows in the moist grass, eyes drowned in a flotilla of freshwater insects, the nape roasted, the heart inundated with rhythms — it's a day of disorder.

Here I am in the middle of my cell, which serves at the same time as bed, office, and Flaubertian screaming room, a square and a desert. I am well, I see myself there, I find my way. The wardrobe sends me back a sparkling twin of precision, heavy with irreplaceable dreams.

The charcoal seller is the master at home. I am the charcoal seller of myself. I feel bound to life & to solitude as the reflection of a willow is bound to a river. And yet free, free with the freedom of the blink of an eyelid.

We understand each other, the "digs" and I. We exchange messages. But — if this universe of books and papers had been put in order, if the Salvation Army had emptied my inkwell of its alcohol, if the Society for the Protection of Animals had filed the teeth of my pen-holders, if the Ministry of Hygiene had signed expulsion orders against ludions, verses, molicases, ceppoits, if I no longer saw, in its circus of light, "babinodant o' the jaw and the gringonassant of teeth," as the goat song is done, the naked demon of free will, I would feel ripe for hara-kiri with a letter opener. Don't touch my stuff! Leave my parents where they are, my memories at my door, my quirks in their place!

I only feel like a man of the future and of love, a citizen of solitude and of sorrow in the midst of my mounds, who is lost in the trammel net of crowds. Dazzling endosmosis allows me to have a light foot, a nimble hand, a sure eye. The hat is housed with books, linen next to literature, the dictionaries roam like millipedes, mille-feuilles, a thousand ideas. My bathrobe gesticulates as if I were still in it. A corner of a blank page gives me the key to my work. I find the Vapex in the middle of the proofs to be corrected. Disorder, all that? No, the elation of the solitary one.

Let me clarify: there is no rule that obliges a man to sleep on his right side, to choose cassoulet from a menu rather than roast pork, to get up to creation at a certain moment. Man is always creating. When Shakespeare was asked where he got the subject of his plays, he replied: "In dreams." So he went to the purest of disorder. He was turning the pages of the wonderful album of nights. He begged determinism to retire with its tray. Order offers mortals pillows. Disorder puts them on the road toward the possible.

Life is not a bouquet of consequences. It's this concert around us, of unexpected explosions, of bells that proclaim, of feelings that are born and die. The pleasures of the spirit are these strangers in hotels, these passing beings, these windows that open, these adventures that are knotted together. Are we not happy at heart, in France, to maneuver through the complication of social events, theatrical enthusiasms, and external anxieties? And isn't it to protect the dislocations from which we derive our wellbeing and our voluptuousness that we order formulas at every moment? And what we desire in our hearts is the regulation of clutter. We want recipes to assimilate disorder. We hear that we are being served traffic permits and potpourri patents.

Disorder is our personality. The desk drawer of this Head of State is his very soul. Start classifying his papers, there is no more Head of State, only an empty chair. This jumbled, asymmetrical ensemble, with squinting books, with blotter paper without tail or head, this mixture of manuscripts and pharmacies, is the place where I extend the branches of my tree and the shadows of my horoscope.

To touch it would be to stab myself in the back. If I alone have the power to find in my labyrinth a penknife, an envelope, an invitation, a razor blade, a magnifying glass, a cork, a hundred-franc note, or the pearl of my evening shirt, it's because I alone in the world have power and know how to be myself. So, peace on earth to men of good incoherence!

High Solitude

Here I am standing before this still life: the mirrored armoire, the bed, the curtain the color of a sad bird, the tears of a cholemic and rainy day on the windows. A little noise from the city seethes at the edge of the building. Caresses of wind, short and hurried, whirl by, like the streaks of crazy fires. The night is a dark factory road. In the distance, on the oilcloth of a deserted street, the shadows of the trees stretch out to sleep.

Yesterday, I was not so far away … I seemed to see more coastlines, a horizon of human heads, to hear the gliding of cars that brushed by my road into darkness. Already today, the crust of the subterranean has drawn closer, deep-sea ghosts crawl with insidious flakes over familiar mysteries, the corner, the doorframe, the recess, the hallway. Sudden eddies make me think that the whole machine kicks off into another existence, that for me there will be new brethren, new former mistresses, new friends at the end of the race. I run to the windows of moving exile. But the distances are consumed. I carry myself like a spoil to the presbyopic portholes pierced into pure eternity. Mirages fade like mist on ice. No silent lighthouse balances on the maggoty road. The city, stuffed with living creatures like blackheads on the face of a pitiable liver, is nothing more than a trifle, a rag of stones, some vague juicy opacity in the midst of which I whirl.

I no longer have earth under my feet. One after another, those who spoke my name under the streetlights, those who opened doors for me, those who smiled at me on the terraces, have fallen. I don't have room anywhere anymore. And life pushes me, gives me support, as if I still had some chance of seeing a long handshake rising like a roadblock...

Life won't let me stop. It does not allow me to build landings in my solitude. I have to come down. My destiny encircles me, already surrounds me, throws me in the direction that it wants, which I will try to understand until the end. All these windows, and every day night approaches... Every day... Every day shuffles the same cards, ends up losing some, in adding new ones, which resemble the others. These descents and ascents, from day to night, like wagons in a quarry, empty me of a necessary sand...

The sole warming moments, the sole maternal prolongations, are the night hours, when, like a mechanic in his boiler room, I work on my solitude, seeking to direct it into the sea of insomnia into which the long line of the dead has thrown us. As you sink into these layers of silence and abandonment, from which we never, never return, we must adopt new habits, find another place for our form. We pass from bark to sapwood, from chitin to heart, from heart to furrow, like the tendril of a coleopteran, paying attention to the slightest gesture, otherwise everything would collapse. This new world, wherein the ink of my inner life dissolves, is similar to a glass cathedral that a too strongly experienced feeling would trample. Among the great solo sailors there is a long-distance captain who has pleased me since my childhood. Today, as I am sailing in my turn, I realize that we must learn to be alone, just as we must learn, like a foreign language, the death of loved ones.

Tonight, a great surf of skeletons and human gusts rescues the skiff. The table is sad, the window languid. The bones of silence creak. I thought that solitude was a sort of supernatural steppe, a great desert of thirst that was further lengthened by interminable delusions. No. It is a mold that tightens, like a wheat field around the body of an abandoned soldier. Solitude, isolation, boredom, these are shovelfuls of emptiness on the path of a mole.

I invent a clock, a barometer, passwords: it is no longer cold for me when it is cold for others. Crowds complain about events that I no longer hear. The newspaper that I'm buying melts in my hands like a donut made of snow. The streets that I take are other streets. The passersby on whom I stumble bristle with problems. Here is another black parcel, then a man alone, then some men with a fat lady, then a solitary young girl. You need only to sit on the terrace of a café to see passersby turning back into beasts. Ah! I didn't know what all this was; I didn't know what was in there! I know it sometimes, for a second, but I can't *stop it*. I sometimes run to meet them. But a siren that I activate, a kind of *Beware of Solitude!* warns them. They flee.

And I, who has not the first *sous* of sleeping fortunes, I am doomed to commute before crowds that no longer see me. Sometimes, I watch the waiters of this café delineate violent curves with ten drinks balanced on their biceps. I see the thinkers at table, hysterical Jews sick with pride, the yawns of the bourgeoisie for whom life is neither more precious nor more eloquent than a pile of handkerchiefs in the immortal armoire. So, I ask the fortress to surround itself with one more wall, to increase itself with an additional density. What tortures has temptation too... Thereupon, I wonder how I was torn from the lives of others. What a flurry, from the moment the first names didn't answer the call! In the beginning was Rue du Colisée, whose façades I often see in images. I return there frequently. Everything died in the change: the door at the end of the courtyard, the stables turning left, the dining room with its stove. And, at the back, to the right, on the street, our two windows with blue curtains. That's it, and it's so old, and it's so close. We stirred in there, I and the others, we were happy there, unhappy … How many millions of ourselves in all the cities, in all the houses, with their kitchens, their faucets, their restless heads, their hearts that light up and darken without anyone being able to see, their head which mixes up its protrusions, its threads, its threads of grooves, its clots of blood, its chalky racks. The heart that starts to jump, to knock on the door … They are all happy, unhappy, with their fingers, their heads falling into the bed full of rage, full of grief, the light off, the morning removing its hat, their body getting dressed, winding up its watch, its little mill of death. And who leaves again, who descends the staircase with great crushing blows, who gets lost, who dissolves in the street. So there you have it … and those damned glances that made us so sad …

Thus, every evening, I welcome my body and I pity it. Tired of having waited for it, patient and without shell, I can barely drag myself to it, I can barely find the fissure through which I will plunge until it is tired. For a revenant less alone and less tested, it seems that things themselves might be agitated. Who is the one a nightmare does not wait for, lurking in the pocket of some room … Me, I wait only for myself. And when my body, all bathed in the city, all juicy from contacts, returns to me, climbing its stairs with effort, I only find in it a flavor of drowning that flows straight down.

Duration keeps me so long among those who are not alone that I see it pass beneath the windows of my room, like the liquid landscape that flows from the trains. For others, duration is immobile. They have time to pay their bills and invent novels. They do not go out on their own. Their brain provides services. They buy love with proverbs, explaining their character, lying, rendering mysterious their rickets and tuberculosis. They invite themselves, they believe in remedies. Everything smiles on them, everything is family, even the voices from *the other room*, those wordless voices that are like the rumbling of dwarf armies ... They go to foodstuffs, to ideas, to emotions, they serve them well, they pack what's been bought, and it is delivered to their homes. But me, I see monsters ...

Where this other sees sincere teeth, soft eyes, half-open books, where the passerby will stretch out along a piece of flesh, like a boat next to another boat, I see nothing but crookbacked yawners, scavenger owls, roly-polies, misoglyphs and grumblers ...

It's been days since I lifted the lid of my hatch. The silent music of nasal grief sounds at the bottom of the turbine. The world has arrived at its minuscule state. I revolve in a thumbnail sketch. The rest of the energy falters, and I wonder who I'm purring with in my enclosure. I am so alone that already I take myself for someone else ...

The world leaves me like the blood of one who opens his veins in a bathtub. And, in the morning, when I approach the gelatinous mirror of some palace room, at that hour when we swear to hold fast, I see myself degraded, without buttons, without epaulettes. Men and women have come before me, who one by one have torn from me feelings, tenderness, and friendly clobberings. What wind has then blown on these chevrons that set poor images whirling?

As far as I see myself in the street, as deeply as I immerse myself in the din of a century, mixed with passersby, clinging to parents, that is to say at the beginning of my poor famous existence from the outside, from this existence of which I'm told so much, when they don't reproach me, what then? ... A child, Faubourg Saint-Honoré, kept on a leash by his mother. That day, I still had the smell of new fabric dye in my nose. I felt like a little girl. And I saw, as I walked, a fat little white cloud above the church of Saint-Philippe-du-Roule. Having departed my comrade Midy's pharmacy on the left, we arrived on the right in front of the Coquelin-Dalloyau Patisserie, which smelled so good, like hot dough. But the veil is still parting ...

It feels like walking through the Alma Market, which rises up from the ruins, one scorching morning, into an expanse of sun, of endless tarmac ...

I also see myself returning home on the arm of my English maid, clean and smooth as a saddle, and who came to fetch me from the Institution with the delightful gait of a crew horse. Here, sometimes, memories overlap, like marbles in a sack. We can't seem to get one out … The Champs-Elysées where I shook my comrades like bells. It was my mother's hand again, one afternoon, in the department store, stroking my sick head. It's the climb up to school, one day, in a long alley of kids, the schoolbag on my back …

These endosmoses between the past and myself, these returns to experience, the gone-by, the ground-down, I am exhausted, I am overwhelmed, I am drunk with them. What cogs went awry in these sequences that I came out of them in the state I'm dressed today? I might have been able to find my way around again, if I had done what as a teenager, I had planned to do: to record every day, every evening, what I had done that day. Perhaps one day I would have discovered, in this sparkling, in this massacre, the drawing of myself, the secret of my mental labyrinth. I would have seen it little by little detach itself, take shape, fix its sensitive formulas, arrange its laws, sharpen its springs. But life already pushes you; tumbles you like sand from a wheelbarrow. Already, your destiny encircles you, encircles you surreptitiously, more and more, closer and closer, puts its finger on your neck, presses you harder and harder, directs you onto the railway that it wants, that you do not want, no arguing, and without consenting that you ever understand a word of your adventures, of your servitude in existence, of your civil service as a man, nothing, nothing, nothing, nothing, never anything, not even the end.

Yes, you should have noticed all this, you should have run behind this avalanche with pen in hand, welding together these smells: smells of the morning, of fiacres, of leg-of-mutton sleeves, of black jerseys, of first couturiers' mannequins, of bread-rolls, of men of the time; the sun's smell of honey, right at the edge of the waxed parquet floor, the worried smell of the street, the smell of concierges, of penurious school principals, of bric-a-brac dealers, of basements, of post offices, the odor of pastilles, the powdery odors of summer drafts, supported by large casks of shadow...

Hélas, all is lost, all is trampled. I know a lot of men feel strongly. Some are magicians and some prophets. Would I have been? Or more simply would I have been sincere? Would I have wanted to say everything, tried to say everything? And then, I was so little aided, so little surrounded, so alone already in a circus of worried faces, studious ears, sad words. I was far too preoccupied with debating the very sources of my poor inner life, rowing around myself, warding off poisoners or ghosts that I sensed, warming life in my own niche, barricading myself with living things, to arm myself with reasons to live. Too preoccupied to take on a surplus. So every time I tried, it was a false start and its procession of somersaults. I was never able to find the springboard, to give the famous foot-feint...

I was advancing into the past. Today, I have nothing more than that, and I hold on to it like an old medal. I turn it into a yellowed diploma. I still revolve in mother images, in memories. And I catch a glimpse at intervals, when the boat threatens to sink, I catch a glimpse, I can clearly see that there is nothing truer than memories. We have spoken very well of matter and memory. There is no first sign of the Universe for us. Those Masters long searched for what today would be without yesterday. The cream of the crop, and a bit more: Taine, Spencer, William James, Bergson. Don't bother with the living, writes Karin...

These are my master keys. The chemistries, the negotiations, the bartering of the most twisted brains are dry, circumscribed, lacking in juice with certain shortcuts, certain ellipses of images, certain seizures, certain distant musical shocks. And then, we have so few ideas below us, scarcely more numerous than the generations. No more variety, no more richness than in the many Meccano combinations that can be made with a small number of letters, with dice or matches, and which can all be reduced to tables, to logarithms, to polynomials. What poverty, what sad evidence, what dusty recipes for the skull of the good wife of Baroness Informé, of Mr. Know-It-All, of Mr. I'm In Experimental Politics, Mr. and Mrs. Shabby!

Tonight, like the other evenings in the chain, it is better to go home, along with the shamelessly, piously extinguished light. No one is waiting for me in the hut. But here, no one is holding me back. I dined at the Dedouluze-Legaillard, merchants of luxury wine and jewelry for the poor. I tasted Baroness *Selfmadegirl*, a buckshee of milk. For a hundred and a hundred years I have dined and dined again between a genius doctor and a syrupy dodo. Here and there, I meet some Nobel Prize for Blackmail, some boudoir alligators, ebonite monstrillons. I shake so many hands I have a collection of fingernails on my conscience. No, I prefer to be alone.

And in the evening too, when coffee is absorbed like a cigarette butt, I prefer my solitude to their intellectual dismissals, to their suros, to their worldly dancers, those spavined horses. My friends, no doubt, yes friends, but in the heap, what shavings, what false witnesses, what false guts! I leave them to their chatting, to their Right, to their Left. I never go to shows. I don't go to theaters, those stations of solitude. I dread the hot embrace of the author, still a friend, no doubt, or of a successful little young man, but whose inspiration is of such a quality that it takes three days to get over it. I love my solitude, like a country house, like a vigilant retreat. The tears that I shed are over.

Yes, walking your own ghost, a comfortable and healthy ghost, a beautiful jellyfish with lambrequins, barely eaten away inside, a brazier under a balaclava, a newly scoured spacesuit that is only oxidized on the other side … Finally, an older brother. But it is late. All I have left is to exchange a few friendly words with the hotel porter, a brave tirailleur too, a good human bastard who can still be counted on. I linger again, before embarking for the night, before going to stand guard around my sleep. If you could know, you who read me, all the art I bring to postpone the moment of going up there, in my geode hotel, like a hermit crab in a foreign shell, like the consciousness of a cave …

Alright, let's go …

Nomadic Spectres

Without being a specialist in moving as some illustrious predecessors were, I flatter myself on knowing what it is like to walk around Paris, furniture on my back, suitcases and silverware in tow. I once left, or better put, we left, and my parents begged me to mind my own beeswax, Rue du Géorama for la Chapelle, that place for Rue du Colisée, the latter for Rue de Dunkerque, Gare du Nord for Passy, Passy for Boulevard Magenta, that for Rue de Saint-Quentin, that for the outskirt Saint-Martin, Gare de l'Est for Rue Château-Landon, two minutes of silence … And I speak here only of the important stages of this panorama of trunks and of wheels, of vans and of shoulders, of pianos and of ropes, which still form the backdrop of certain dreams …

The move is a *Romanichel* drama that one plays out on one's own, sans audience, in a restricted, literary domain, suddenly called to become a Fingal's grotto, a Vulcan's workshop. All of a sudden, when you begin to roll in the shape of a giant cigarette some carpet cut to your floors, you feel that the world is spinning, that the earth is round, that there is in the shadow of our senses a mineralogical, teratological universe, that spiders live in comfort, that mirrors breathe, that chairs have knees, and armoires breasts.

Here is a mouse with a cunning muzzle, seated on its butt, as sharp as the pillar of a seraglio, as Benjamin Rabier saw it, and which thinks, as Jules Renard wanted. Here is the Walt Disney moth, which begins a six-day round from the top to the bottom of our ghostly gesticulations: it no longer finds the solid cloth overcoat on which its family lived, the way an assembly of peasants lives on a ham; it no longer sees, neither the great felt sport hat it was pecking for its dessert, nor the pair of lined gloves, nor the streaky curtains, nor the blotting paper cravats. It's the world turned upside down!

Thin geysers of purple dust, curved and serrated like ferns, smoke from the divans like a Carlos Schwabe watercolor. A few woodlice in chainmail scurry toward their humid barracks; century-old flies emerge from their bands and fiddle with heavy flight before perishing on the windowsills, where they fall like drops of ink. Mustaches detach from Harlequin masks, ants gallop along bathroom tracks. Meanwhile the cockroach, which is part undertaker, part miniature penguin, and part hearse of the insane, paces, slow and sulky, like a melancholy pawn, the kitchen tiles.

One fine morning, the first crate arrives. Will it be books, knick-knacks, souvenirs, useless items, shirts or table linens? We confer, and we end up leaving it to the insensitive specialists, to their rubber band moves, the care of plunging your things into dark and fragile abysses. During this time, your furniture rises, like a tide of huge cigars. Already, you are obliged to climb onto a chair, which is itself balanced on a chest, to wash your hands, and it's not a piece of soap that you find in its damp and traditional place, but a cremone, an umbrella, or the saber of the grandfather who was an artillery captain of the 31st Horse Mounted Hunters.

Today, it's a beloved neighborhood that I leave, this mosaic formed by Boulevard Saint-Germain, Rue de Buci, and Rue du Four. In that area I found myself in the middle of Parisian brains. I felt besieged by bookstores, surrounded by painters, toil, dreams, spirituality. But time appears, once again, in the navel of *the* pendulum, in the meshes of my horoscope: the suitcases must be taken down, the trunks dusted, the cufflinks thrown into the carriage, which has become a limited company, the sleeve buttons, the dear accumulated memories, the brushes, which, with eyes closed, feel like the backs of foals or the flanks of an ornithorhynchus; art magazines, shoetrees with the condyles of athletic intellectuals; flannel pants and heavy literature, dictionaries, corrected proofs, bills, ashtrays, etc. ...

The people from Cook's or from Bedel's, from Duchemin's or from Borniol's, are entering, with sad eyes and dangling arms. Because a move always feels like a funeral. Already, I see a hundred elbows, bundles of legs. I no longer know where to put myself. The telephone resounds in this camp, thundering like a war siren: some friends believe I've returned, sometimes they confuse me with another, some Léon-Paul who would be a dentist or a gonfalonier. Then, there is the problem of mail: should we pay a visit to the postmaster of the post office in my neighborhood, leave instructions at the hotel I am vacating, or return every day on pilgrimage, hands behind my back, heart full of romantic regrets? Should I write a little card and send it to everyone who can write to me? What if I forget, if they throw that card in the trash, among the packages of razor blades and empty cigarette boxes?

It is also advisable to address a last smile to the merchants of the place of which I shall no longer be a familiar shadow: the pharmacist, Mr. Douce, the dry cleaner, Mr. Quinche, the hairdresser, Mr. Roques, the newspaper merchant, Mme. Chateau, the tavern-keeper, the shoemaker, the chauffeurs, at least the ones I know ...

The first nailed, tied, or welded crates are already gliding toward new regions. In this one I can see the corpse of my tuxedo, which forms a mass grave with a vase, a telephone from 1902, sock-garters that wriggle like dowels. In this other, the remains of a writing table, curled up between underwear and half curtains. O wandering coffins, where things sleep with a brief sleep, like men, before experiencing the joys of eternal life, which, for them, is resolved by moving in …

Here a remark comes to mind that I offer without further delay to novelists: a relocation consists of two acts: the actual relocation, and the move-in, that is, the rebirth, the resurrection, the creation of the world under other skies. Yet, in the case of chinoiseries that have remained secret, the passengers use, when they have to talk about this complicated operation, only one phrase. They say: *I have relocated.* Why? Undoubtedly, for us other mortals so fond of secrecy, the move-in involves a series of shameful or seraphic pleasures, which we intend to keep secret. Hence this axiom: to relocate is to die, to move-in is to love.

Another joy to be derived from these journeys from neighborhood to neighborhood is the feeling of rejuvenation. Happiness, I don't know which philosopher murmured in the last century, consists in knowing how to constantly forget lost happiness. So with youth. Let us continuously forget lost youth and we will succeed in not growing old. I feel I have the legs of an urchin, to follow on the stairs those who carry my shoes away, toward the Montrouge of my childhood, my shoes, my Larousse, my Quicherat, my Alexandre, my spinet, my revolver, my past and my heart. The room that I leave is no more than a desert of monotony where the walls take on the colors of solidified clouds. The demons of solitude, with thighs like long grasshoppers, tunnel-colored eyes, dance on the steps of silence, while I abandon the last things in my bag: shaving cream, eau de cologne, matches, a penholder, a toothbrush, and the day's newspaper, which come to greet me here for the last time.

Ah! don't try to tell me man is not a vagabond, still rich with a twenty year old soul!

The Death of the Ghost

It was in my opinion a very peaceful street before the arrival of the ghost, of "Monsieur le Fantôme," as my concierge said, who had been led to believe that there were many kinds of ghosts: rich and poor, good and bad. And, with the brave intention of reassuring herself, she added, when handing me the catalog of the Galeries Lafayette and the subscription form for the Work of the Orphans of Mont-de-Piété, "He is not as devilish as he is black!"

In vain did I explain to her that it was necessary to distinguish that there were devils, and the Devil, revenants, ghosts, apparitions, spirits, lemurs, gnomids, gavalouses, colbassons, and perfidious crivanosses, which have human nails, frog hair, and the reticences of old racehorses. The good woman did not allow herself to be convinced.

"The ghost, that's what in my house we call the Devil," she said. "Call it whatever you like, it's still the same. First of all, you only have to ask Monsieur Droiturier, since he saw it."

Yes, it was a street such as we hardly see anymore. Gentle, welcoming, always ready to console you when you return from long walks, healthy, not afraid of rain, nor posters, nor work. And then one day, a certain Monsieur Droiturier, an orphan in number

18, who lived in a small attic room, all alone, and who earned 750 francs a month with an iron merchant shoveling filings into wagons, Droiturier, to whom the concierge said "Monsieur," as if to a ghost, because he played cards in a servants' quarter, because he sometimes came home by taxi, that Monsieur Droiturier had seen, one evening, as he was walking back from the cinema, a spectre.

"Something white & fast. Something like a swift moving cloud, a cloud that would be afraid of arriving late for a storm …," explained to me a former actor who had opened a dye shop under my windows. He himself had not seen the thing, but, from the very first he had offered to consolidate the descriptions of the inhabitants of the street.

"I have always believed in apparitions," he added, "as I believe in volcanic eruptions & gold mines, but I have never witnessed such phenomena. Yet, as far as the ghost of Monsieur Droiturier is concerned, he had passed so close to this store that I cannot doubt it. 'He would even have brushed against my door,' said Monsieur Droiturier. Transparent, bouncy, sometimes thin, like good cigar smoke in a place where there is a slight draft, he walked just like a man. Who knows if you or I did not take him for a stray pedestrian?"

A week later, we spoke only of that revenant. Some had seen it emerge from a manhole, as the

Mephistopheles of *Faust* does in the theater; others had seen him exiting a taxi, settling his fare, and entering number 23 on tiptoe, allowing the partisans of the third theory to claim that it was a woman, and that the dentist of 23, whose legitimate wife spent half her life in the hospital, was quite free to take another. Pushed against the wall, these commentators had no difficulty in recognizing that there was no manhole in that part of the street, and that the dentist led an irreproachable life. Like everyone else, they spoke just to speak, and because it is not clever, simple people think, to stand silent before the supernatural.

Alone, Monsieur Droiturier said nothing. When we pressed him with questions, he would reply that he had seen the ghost crossing the street and that he had nothing more to add. We invented a thousand stratagems to make him talk: the wine merchant called him to offer him an aperitif, the milkman offered him credit, the butcher notified him that he set aside, for his delight, his most tender rib eyes. Coachmen lingered in the street, wishing to see this character appear before number 18, made of shaving cream or blancmange, who had not yet had, according to them, time to escape. The great news had its own momentum.

Monsieur Droiturier was content to see. The others were determined to describe, to clarify, to pull dreams from their memory to oppose the new-comer with the old ghosts of their youth. They were hardly listened to, the best of the attention on the street having been absorbed by the recent spectre. Because the past didn't matter. And the belief gradually established itself, sinking into the substance of the buildings, as in a season. Those who tried to escape it were reminded of the feeling of reality by the cracking of a pan in the middle of the night, by the abrupt stoppage of clocks, the disappearance of a fire iron, or the unexpected ring of the bell by a delivery boy who was at the wrong door …

Then came a period of canal-smelling rains, covering the windows with zebra striped patterns, with splashes of sky, with tears, which facilitated these suppositions. In the evening, before sneaking past their hot wives, the men believed they were on the trail of the goblin. Clouds raced along windows with the rapidity of spiders. Trucks seemed to creep under houses like moles and shake them. The concierges of the forty-six buildings on the street met one day at a wine merchant's, under the pretext of participating in a card tournament, la manille, and searched in vain for a method. The ghost was nothing more than a whisper, thunderclap, lightning, black cat, foreboding, siren howl. He refused to show himself a second time in the guise of a real ghost. In vain did we wait for him just where Monsieur Droiturier had seen him, for he remained invisible.

In the evening, when I went down to the street, I found it smelt of trampling, a taste of wet shoes, of pants simmering in the rain that sang to me in all the tones that we had expected, queuing for hours, its throat tightened with a desire for a ghost. I saw, standing before their shops, the coal seller, the cobbler, the grain trader, whose long, shining shadows stretched out over the granite of the pavement like the shadows of poplars. The street, with all its windows lit, swayed heavily like an ocean liner. The sea was calm, dense. The salad & banana merchant was putting her ping-pong table back under an archway with dirty caryatids. A few taxis followed one another like the noise of a sawmill. At the crossroads, a tramway moved with difficulty like a carnival chariot through a grove of onlookers.

The radio, the phonograph, and the cries of children with sugared erythema united in a cachexiatic, sickly concert, which, filtered through the wallpaper, the lost linen, the poorly locked window, was scattered in the middle of the street like the barrel organ music of Barbary. Everyone wanted to throw two *sous* into the apartments. Workmen kept looking for reasons not to return home until half-an-hour, an hour later. They remained standing in the prune compote of this winter's end, a quarter kilo of brie in their pockets, their eyes moist and curious, like one from whom blinders had been removed...

Housewives hung from windows, with Bastille Day hair, goiters, and linen flapping like bats. Chalky girls pretended they were shopping in the neighborhood and stretched their tetanic necks as they ran down the street. The old men murmured in their sweaty sheets, demanding herbal teas, deafness, agonies. They were reassured that the ghost, or the vampire, or the petrogale with espadrilles, the phylloxera on a bicycle, the matamata, the forked gorgon, was finally going to escape from a lantern, come out of an ear, manifest above a mess of soup. And the old men fell back into a half-sleep already impregnated with hell.

I walked in a sort of nasal halo made of whispers and lights. The street was heavy on my shoulders like grief. It was palpitating. It had welcomed movements from cellars and roofs. It had no milieu, no center, no cohesion. The carpenter was no longer at home, between 5:00 & 7:00, as since the assassination of Concini, the laundress regularly gave me two police officer's handkerchiefs and a diver's shirt in whose fabric mandarin-curaçao disputed with chlorine. The window of the expert accountant, which guided me through the night, didn't light up until three-quarters of an hour later, the old man having decided to treat himself to an aperitif meditation before returning home.

I guessed that the whistling of men, which grazed carriage doors like bullets, was no longer a love call, that the girls were kissed with their ears at attention and their eyes open so as not to miss the leprechaun. The way you don't dare read a newspaper if you're waiting for your beloved's phone call. Even if you sit next to the device and stroke it like a cat, it will not calm the racing of your heart. You need a ring, to survive.

Now, the street demanded its ghost.

Already, we were beginning to murmur about the passage of Monsieur Droiturier. Had he seen it as he said he did? It was difficult to doubt his word. Monsieur Droiturier hardly drank and never got angry. Nor was it possible to see why he would have invented a spectre. But good souls asserted that, if he'd actually seen it, he should have kept it to himself. The spectre was believed to be suffering from agoraphobia. It was suspected of avoiding publicity. Incredible nonsense circulated about it. Any more of this, and we would have turned it into a farce.

The street began to sulk. The dying wasted their time, births became difficult. A gas explosion occurred at 33, leaving in the middle of the sidewalk an enormous cavity full of lobster legs. It was a serious, strange injury. And we couldn't help but think that the ghost was behind it. He had taken vengeance on incredulity. Monsieur Droiturier who, for several days, had not spoken to anyone, rushed to meet people, as if to reassure them, as if to defend the one who passed for his accomplice.

But, in secret, he rejoiced at the gas sneeze, the black abscess, all boiling with caviar, which had reminded his neighbors that ghosts are as powerful as engineers. My concierge advised me to move. A sheet music merchant, who kept a shop under a carriage entrance, died while humming the *Valse Brune*, and permission was required from the police commissioner to remove his products, which he fixed on ropes with clothespins. Measles swept through apartments like a drum roll. One of the municipal councilors of the arrondissement, who lived at 27, perhaps the sole person of the great troubled family who had always refused to believe in the apparition, lost his position at the Town Hall.

Monsieur Droiturier triumphed. Often, returning home at dawn, I would see him from my window, going off to work, robust and audible. He did not have his ghost with him, but he was rich with it, he was radiant. He seemed to dispose of it as country squires dispose of their land, sell, build, invite, without having the least atom of that earth in their pocket. One evening, I had the idea of whistling with my fingers and hiding myself before he looked up. The noise went off like a lasso and nearly tied up Monsieur Droiturier, who immediately began to scamper off without looking back. His gallop roused a few inhabitants of the street who were no more than three or four seconds away from the sound of their alarm clocks. Skylights opened. I saw disheveled heads appear along the houses, as at the windows of express trains ...

In the evening, my concierge informed me that Monsieur Droiturier had not returned.

— How do we know?

— This morning, we saw him run away. We thought that he'd stolen something. The baker, who just had a casserole pot to fix, went to see her boss. Monsieur Droiturier was not there. No one had seen him.

— He'll be home later; he's having fun ...

— Oh! no. I'm sure that he's taken off.

— Taking his ghost along, I ventured.

— Perhaps, said the good woman.

Then, having been struck by what was so profound in her answer, she clarified:

— He ran off with his ghost.

The night passed without incident. When questioned later by a police inspector in charge of the Fantastic, some residents claimed to have heard the whirring of an airplane engine. Information gathered about military or commercial formations, no aircraft had been able to fly over Paris that day. For his part, the butcher asserted that, far from being explained by a jet, the buzzing they heard could only be terrestrial, and signified a truck or taxi. This mystery still persists.

We lived a week in uncertainty. Newspapers leapt on the thing like fishermen on sardines, and published that a certain Monsieur Droiturier, a laborer by trade, had disappeared quite mysteriously from his room, from his house, from his street, and undoubtedly from his neighborhood, after having frightened the population by pretending that a ghost inhabited the environs. That evening, I thought I heard in a dream the first tinklings, the first tramplings, of a Crusade. It was still admitted that Monsieur Droiturier had disappeared, but there was no doubt cast on the apparition. This spectre was the monument of the district, its *Song of Roland*, its Obelisk, its Declaration of the Rights of Man. A joker having risked on the zinc bar top the opinion that Monsieur Droiturier and the ghost were one, or rather — a vision —, was nearly lynched in the middle of the bar.

But word caught on. Who was this Monsieur Droiturier? The housewives approached each other, happy and yet bored at being able to parry at leisure a man who had lived in their wake, who had put his feet where they placed theirs, and who, perhaps, might no longer be alive. Murderer, beneficiary of some jackpot, caught up in the cinema, classified as a druid or gold-maker, they might have forgotten him. But, the friend of a ghost … Was it possible to drive him from memory? They invented a life for him at once attractive and perverse. Young girls passed by, rouged and mannered, applying their uterine genius to make the street believe that they had shared the bed of the deceased. All the men in the neighborhood had played cards with him.

One evening as I was going to the Opera, I saw a gathering in front of the house already emblazoned with a commemorative plaque. I was in full regalia. Struck by curiosity, I elbowed my way into the small group to get to the front row. My outfit surprised the onlookers, who mistook me for the magician called in for consultation, and they pushed me into the building without even giving me time to protest. I was going up. The long staircase was rotting with the stench of pipe tobacco and cervelas. All the tenants at their doors greeted me, mingling with their gestures a strange relief, a kind of breathing-prayer reserved for Lamaist priests.

Finally, I made it to the 8th floor. The door to the attic in which Monsieur Droiturier had lived was open. The room was empty. Three men stood in the middle. I joined them without surprising them. The best dressed, who could only be the police commissioner, greeted me discreetly with an air of circumstance, probably taking me for a relative of the missing person. For a long time we remained silent looking at the walls of this immaculate little room, without furniture, without stains, in which swirled, with the purest silence, a snow squall of flashing moths…

To overcome the uneasiness which, bit by bit, enveloped us, one of the companions of the man whom I took for a police commissioner murmured, in a childish voice:

"He won't have known what to become, with his ghost, and probably killed himself somewhere."

— First of all, said the spectator, the ghost is not an object likely to be stolen. Secondly, theft or, to speak correctly, the abduction of a phantom does not constitute a crime.

— I am for suicide, Chief, said the man who had spoken first.

— The most curious, replied the Chief, after reflecting for a moment, the most curious thing about this story is that, from the information that I could obtain, the man named Droiturier probably never lived in this house. You will tell me that the whole street, starting with the owner of the building, claims the opposite. You'll tell me that Monsieur Droiturier has shaken hands, bought provisions, received letters. I will tell you that that is not enough for me.

— If, however, even admitting that, presumably, unless we can suppose …, said someone who had not yet opened his mouth …

But the Commissioner, for he was indeed the Commissioner, cut him short. We saw him reflecting by himself, pulling out his eyebrow hairs without flinching, which no doubt he only did under certain obscure circumstances. Then he said:

— Follow me. I have an idea. In your presence I'm going to ask a crucial question of the crowd.

We went downstairs, pushing each other, the steps soft as gums. Standing in the same place, the tenants seemed out of breath. Sensing some declaration was forthcoming, they followed suit. On arriving at the ground floor, there were a hundred of us. Finally, the Commissioner stopped, looked with a parliamentary eye at the crowd facing him, quickly constructed a clear sentence that he did not intend to repeat, raised his head, and asked:

— Come, my friends, had any of you known Monsieur Droiturier before the appearance of the ghost?

No one answered.

Then the Commissioner turned to us and, in a slightly provocative tone, murmured:

— You see!

Naturally, I missed the first act of *Tristan* that evening.

The Wait

The family includes the father, the mother, the ascendants and their spouses, the descendants and their spouses, the servants ...

A train passes, then another, then another again. The shadow curled up like a fetus above the boiling skulls of the rails. Riddled with black arteries and sooty blood kidneys, the stovepipe unwinds, like an intestine, in the waiting room buffet of a train station, lively as a catchy tune. And when the fast trains pass through our bodies, the stovepipe gently shakes its squamous tin basset fur.

My life sits right in the middle, the past leaning against the red-hot iron, the future turned toward the future in the direction of the trains rushing headlong toward death. For us who are there, lurking, vertebrae flirting with the flames, these dazzling and disdainful trains are women without memory. Frightful or seductive beings that attack us, that in the process snatch some snippet of ourselves. Women are patient and cruel like Sioux. And the life of us men, our share of ardor and trust, has been used for a hundred and a hundred years for their trampling and their puzzles. Fashion merchants, daughters of water and forest inspectors, arrive in Paris, finger in nose, callus visible under their first patent leather, sometimes a Jew in the background who has been pushing them into existence for a century. They organize themselves, carefully part the curtains with tiebacks, distinguish the newcomer from the wealthy man, ravage destinies, impose their dogs, their lovers, clamber to storm social events, as if on a pile of dry leaves, suffocating under their hurried heels the poor buggers all smoldering with hope and bravery. Then, tongues reach out toward these monsters of innocence, toward these horrible virginities. Flowers flock by every path, the sexes form a hedge along their path, drumming celebrates an infinity of authoritarian pleasures. And we arrive, with the aid of some husband who is as cuckolded as he is hardworking, as heavy in the stomach as he is hard of hearing, we succeed in imposing the banal, the adulterated, the icy chestnut, the kettle pot poem, the short play, speaking without images, a kind of infusion of snobbism in which, however vigorous, hearts have been burnt alive.

And then, one fine day, these women become doe, skis, flying pools, chirpings of racing starlings, and fast trains. Progress transports them before the frightened men of the suburban stations. They glide with an agile paw on the wires of the telegraph, insult with their knees the dreamless earth of the atrocious countryside, pierce the ceiling, and descend to your very depths, O young lover, like foul, inverted, and frozen mercury.

I came here without my records, lost, exhausted, my legs in my mouth, my soul planted like a spear in the midst of a solid and pale river, seeking in what crease of furniture I could well have forgotten the pieces of my heart. And how can I now get on that painful bicycle that I see dying at my feet, pink under the pink lances of a pink fire? The deputy chief of this station carries his spirit on his chest, like a calendar, with the lies in red. He opens his mouth to announce that swarms will lie down on the tracks of his service. And it's the loudspeaker that captures the words that he speaks.

How I would like to speak to him of my happiness, to this man without eagles and without thirst. Yes, to wrest him away from his destiny, which is to comment on trains as captions are put under drawings, and whisper to him of considerable distresses. His magnificent magick lantern from the toy department struck, as if a lighthouse beam, the walls laden with images and phrases in the breakfast room where our bodies huddle together, one against the other, like lumps of coal, and wear themselves out like large pastilles of veal pâté ...

I see that we have to lose weight and start conquering the Globe again, Thomas Cook brochures in hand. Because we knew nothing before the explorations of the traveling salesmen. I see that we must dress and wash ourselves: there is soap, buckets for fairy hands and nymph linen. Nothing for the poor. The salesman always assumes that women shed tears of silver, that everything is ravishing, right down to the nests of mice behind stoves. I read that beauty has a history, and history a beauty. We are born horrible and we become beautiful. We are born without tar, without soot, without abscesses. And we die with the corpse of a woman between the gums, the body gnarled on its legs like an oak tree. Anxious and industrial gondolas stagger on lakes of blood. What, death already? While so many posters will hold out on this plaster! And the ten fast trains per day that put dreams at twenty francs a pound, pleasure within everyone's reach … What will become of us on the other side of the cylindrical projection of Mercator? In what state will we reach the zone of collapse beyond which no hope of resurrection is allowed? And when it's still 4 o'clock in the middle of Great Bear Lake, 8 A.M. in Formosa, when the weavers of Angers will continue to make in Paris laws in Paris about conduct, adultery, and dignity, while the happiness of life will flow from every volcano as edible lava, what will become of us, poor lovers, at the bottom of the mouthless egg?

… Stations of ashes and sands, how many affronts have come to strike at my attentive carcass, whilst the torrent of lost trains poured between the partitions of France … How many greying hours were scattered on my knees, while I implored those who ought to have stopped here and lived, and put my poor life back together, and nevertheless endeavored to get to the top. How many cramps grew their ivy around my impassive legs, always ready to serve like old horses, their master twisted with confidences and regrets …

… All of a sudden, the arachnid-man slips between the banquettes and proclaims the Brétigny line of Vendôme, the Vierzon, the Argenton-sur-Creuse, the Ostende, the Menton, the Culmont-Chalindrey, changes at Dijon, at Cologne, at Sperme, at Tournebride. A universe of ankles and baskets immediately stirred. The advertising spots dissolve in a battalion of sleepers united like glutinous sardine candies. The bellowing of oxen promises Villettes to furtive half-sleeps. I get up to mechanically follow those who are leaving. But I don't know where I'm going. I don't understand why I should go north rather than south, and why I don't wait here, between these cupboards of impatience, for another convoy.

I am thousands of myself fleeing. And I see myself wandering, hands heavy with suitcases, in the middle of a crossroads of exile where an interchangeable people are left to boil. The groups extracted from their slumber of coal slowly start to travel their politics, to goulafange social issues, to rehash quarrels, filling the soul with equations. A sourpuss asks me for my ticket, leaning over me like the shadow of a pole. And for him I extract from my pocket a piece of paper scrambled with nightmares. I raise my eyes to this feudal servant: his forehead is full of caravans of elephants, his eyelashes in bundles, the track of his lips traversed by trains. I can rarely consider someone without pitying them. And I pity that magnifying eye that fixes itself upon my right of visa.

We have not yet arrived at dawn, and yet the steamer trunk of night rushes forward, mixing us pell-mell, people of banquettes and drinks that nothing disturbs in the depths of their basements. What have I come here to do in this station, since I'm not yet where I will suddenly find, on the verge of exile, all I've been missing? The past, the friends, the forgotten rendezvous', the gentle journey from the café to the grave and from the grave to the café, smiles and lies, the cries of children, and the distraught gestures of all those who have died, of all those who have abandoned me in the middle of stairs, depriving me of their comforting shadow; promises and remorse, crumpled pages and never written letters, assurances and handshakes, a whole sea of lived life, an ocean of moments as close as a deck of playing cards, sighs and anger, immanent anxieties, the great noise of tramways and slippers, a lifetime of boarding houses, apartments and hotels, astonishments and confidences, arms around the neck and legs knotted in the thickness of feverish beds, lamps, sluices, and rest and fatigue, all this weighs on my traveler's siesta...

But She will come. The two of us, we will spend days and weeks, even here, surrounded by baskets and umbrellas. Even here, summoned to jump by the slightest locomotive, we will imagine Buttes-Chaumont, Canal Saint-Martin, the leap-frog of the metro and the sugar of the Sacré-Cœur. Even here, we can embrace each other and push the horrible terminus toward other stations.

It is she, perhaps, my sad deliverance, which at this moment is pushing open the glass door as fragile as a fountain. Is she the one who looks around for the night swimmer, all chilly with apprehension and fervor? No, not yet. It's a ghost without a ticket which has crept toward us, a ghost of a woman whose love had not ended, who still has tears and arms which implore, and whom the other world had no use for. She must finish her journey before returning to the wombs of humans without eyes or movements.

To wait. We must wait more, without watching the hours pass, closing our eyelids to deceive the always-watchful soul. It is necessary to blush under a blanket of men, to warm up to their great shudder of unconsciousness, to be sprinkled with hatred and mediocrity, to focus your hungry attention on the posters of the closed world, the stockings, the summits, the herbal teas, the giraffes, the rolling library that sleeps like a galley kitchen by digesting its printed merchandise. Years will pass. And new years will present themselves. And sometimes I will feel within me, in the midst of a desert of minutes, a great uproar of freshness and hope. And sometimes, I will still hear, like this evening, the uninterrupted footsteps of parades of spectres and the music of toad circuses. Then I will see joys and tears dissolve. And I will cross silently through long spaces without men and without sidewalks, in closed and icy cities where my hovering and swimming heart will have led me.

I am not happy. All these outstretched hands from the waiting room reaching for unknown hands, smiles in their fingernails, disdain me. They go to those who need neither flesh nor heat. They forget this uprooted man who maybe sits up waiting, his back to the stove, his legs enervated, he torn and cursed. I wasn't cut out for distress. Nostalgia was not my métier. But when very young, they wanted to put me in a studio of sadness, and I took the path. I was shown the tools of misfortune, the files of cockroaches, the planes of boredom, the transmission belts of agitation and remembrance. They taught me to connect my heart to other hearts, to expect much from men. I have been taught to present to women only the weakest part of myself. And I have gradually become a professional guy who knows his stuff well. My God! Why didn't they teach me about happiness!? It would have been so simple, while they were at it. And I didn't expect today, crucified to placards, devoted to schedules, for the girls of the past and the impossible to come running to me, in boisterous and stupid but happy circles.

I wasn't cut out for waiting either. I once believed in my childhood bed that things succeeded one another like hours on clock dials, that one event announced another, that rain was a chapter like fine weather, and that the whole formed a book without traps. But I was placed at a young age in the hands of those who reveal the abysses and the lacunas. Since that day, in my dreams, how many doors have remained open, how many unanswered letters, sent telegrams that have fallen dead en route like partridges! I saw thresholds as I waited for clearings. I saw drowned people on canals instead of reflections. I drank tears from glasses when I believed I would find honey. No longer was anything ivory, rainbow, dew, or oath, but muddy paths, turned backs, evil eye and trip-ups. And now it all ends between two trains, in one of those cracks where the meager courage we still had in our pocket is engulfed. Now they crumble, the walls of life between which we groped. All these travelers that rise up to bury me under the joys I've never had, while these others tip the cap of friendship, all the false friends, all the false poets, the false consumers, the false mortals, the false passersby from my unraveled film. I saw nothing but the seepage of my own nonchalance, scraping a little satisfaction from the bottom of the pot, laughing as one coughs, and saying happy new year to the shadows of shadows that accompany me along the grassless trench.

It rises from this twisted station like a mouth of rustling metal and arteriole spasms. A life of iron and axles replaces the emotions, the prudences, the plans. Nothing could be born of that iron paradise before which to sketch supreme genuflections. Man is lost no matter what he does. Unbridled machines rush us in black heaps toward an accelerated becoming, without sky, without curves, closed like a box, a sort of coffin as vast as a Goetheanum in which to shut ourselves up by the millions with all the inhabitants of the earth and all the inhabitants of its soul.

Here is the day. A fresh, rhythmic paint slips from the rooftops toward the brains, cleaning the ducts of the nose and the ear, the rims of the eyelids where sleep has stuck its stamp, and the armatures and the hinges. The passing trains look like trains. No matter how far I turn my head upside down, I cannot find my troupe of dreams, which I parade around like a pawn. If my solitude escapes me in turn, I am lost. The station lamps fall one after the other like ripe pears in a scrap metal orchard. Women and men speak strangely around me. I am at home, at the edge of rails that emerge shiny and comfortable from my own chest. I am at home, surrounded by provincials and baggage, besieged with black coffee, the sole and final vestige of the night. Night juice that the hands of slaves have collected drop by drop in the glass of the desperate.

Azazel

Non adeo est bene nunc ut sit mihi gloria curæ ...
Ovid, *Tristia*, v.12.41[1]

I am neither a philosopher, nor a theologian, nor a partisan. Perhaps I am only a poet because of the drama of seeing physiognomies and facades dying around me. I would like to be nothing but an overcoat thrown over my old soul, and trotting with my bag of tender mischiefs and my box of regrets through these apartments which are the big cities and countries in which I have traveled. When I was the age of those who whistle back and forth from their mothers to their professors, ideas flew to me. The taste for having a life of the senses filled my lungs with a propelling vapor. The approach to the arts & intellectual combinations made me shudder. For women, all that ... I can live today on a bed of beech leaves and carve atrocious drawings on the spotted skin of trees. May all that which is possible remain possible for others. I no longer expect to see the silhouette of God appear in a dazzling niche on a street corner. No barricade makes my hair stand on end.

1. Now things are not so good for me that I yearn for glory.

As I walked to meet myself, I saw myself in the sky-filled mirror of a tailor. If, to die, I had slipped into one of his corkscrew suits until the hot butter of the firebomb rendered everything questionable, we would have seen nothing but fire. I am afraid of what is printed and of what is said. I'm afraid of what people think. I would like to have no more familiarity than with those things that no one invents: raw materials, people in the métro, a few friends who never get vexed. I love the nocturnal terraces where a desperate person comes to you with everything he needs to write under his fingernails and sincerity spreading over him like blood.

How many writers, how many philosophers, and I have the names of some of them on the tip of my tongue, have accustomed us lately to consider with a less distracted and less hasty eye the infinitely small things of our soil! They boasted to us of the signs of all duration and all prosperity: the boat, the ladder, milk, the farm, the hedge, the wheelbarrow, the millstone, the ear of corn. Danger has made us tender for what does not die. We focused on the possibilities of happiness; we raised the level of what the infallible Larousse calls the Laborious Classes. Just images, all that. Good intentions drawn from commonplaces. But still abstractions. The deep ailment from which I suffer hovered like powder in our discussions. Yet, one must have a taste for one's fellow men as one has the cult of the dead …

Where are they, those who have watched me live since I had legs? Ah! how many times have I realized, not without terror, that it's for them alone that I love to write. Not one of them ever suggested that I think like him. We were living, what! And when we exchanged impressions, it was never to try to be witty. We were slightly above the level of plants. We had brains squeezed into a thousand folds of laughter, hearts to guide us. Even today, what deep secrets bind me to the traveler in my compartment who carries in his eyes a naive and legible fate like the design of a tie, with the fisherman on the same bank, the next guy on the café terrace, the client in the same hotel! This ironmonger, this seamstress, this soldier, this cook, this harvester, it is with them too that I walk without hypocrisy toward the river locks of death. And here we are, all lined up on the same line of turf, where the kick-off will be given toward a future without folding screens.

… During the Day, at Night, a few sips of those tons of café au lait that we absorb in a lifetime, the rain, the mud, and the suns, the oaths that run aground, the men who remake History, while the thinnest of the rivers do not change place … Heads are cut here; there we plant forests of cannons. We try to believe that people are not fields of wheat. We organize peace, war, heroism. We get together as if for a funeral, and we rack our brains looking for hymns. But you will always need umbrellas, iodine, salt. And whoever, later, will have swept all this away in his turn, will be distracted by a head cold. At times, I wonder if men will not one day try to tackle rotation, gravity, dew, eternal snow... Let us therefore suffer in peace behind our windows. How I'm here, alone, with my years folded tightly away in my wallet, and I have known nothing more exciting than racing with my family through Paris! Monarchs, artists, women's-men and idea-men have died since this youth! And yet, nothing strikes me as sweeter, more lasting, than these memories. I have felt them a hundred times, these *Romanichel* emotions. A hundred times I have drawn endless dreams from them. Deep down, I never liked what is abstract, what is theoretical, what is talkative. The great idea, the great play, the great opera, the great machine, the great words, the genius of this son of Romatour, who makes comedies for domestic dogs, if it isn't thesis books for dull thinkers, that is to say dinner music, all that doesn't impress me. That's not for me. I prefer the simple ones who watched us tramping the arrondissements, my family and myself, during those happy years.

Ah! I can boast of knowing what it is like to travel around in my kingdom with these trucks that are the bastards of our stagecoaches of old... But I have already told you the driving theme of my poem:

"I once left, or better put, we left, because my parents rarely asked me what I thought of it, Rue du Géorama for la Chapelle, that place for Rue du Colisée, the latter for Rue de Dunkerque, Gare du Nord for Passy, Passy for Boulevard Magenta, that one for Rue de Saint-Quentin, that one for Faubourg Saint-Martin, Gare de l'Est for Rue Château-Landon. Two minutes of silence … And I speak here only of the important stages of this panorama of trunks and of wheels, of vans and of shoulders, of armoires and of ropes, which still form the richest subject of the choice of dreams that I put aside for my old age. And often, between dog and wolf, in some 18th-century brasserie where prewar women hang like hams, we go and dream about all this together, like playing manila, a few old grunts and me."

The café terrace of friends allows the fusion of anger, ambitions, classes and professions: the entrepreneur invites his secretary, who himself prays at his table, with the authorization of his boss, some frigate captain, some colonial met by chance, or some clerk of a notary called to Clichy by poetry … Some hearts are in throats, business is transacted, oaths are exchanged, orders are placed, all things that we didn't think about but that we will never forget, because the coffee of the Labadens is still the best of the marmite pots that we've invented to cook memory.

I've always had the quirks of an old sultan. I imposed involuntary & affectionate, but perfect delays

on my friends. I stayed in bed for weeks, between
my phone and some croissant that was getting as
hard as granite. For other years I lived like a gypsy
between the studio of Vulcan and the cave of Fingal,
nourishing myself on the purple dust of pregnant
locomotives, encountering, in secret restaurants like
harlequin skulls, some shapely and lacey women, like
ferns. I collected "little days" as aviators collect flying
hours. I frequented the great pimps of the Wepler
and the office of Alfred Vallette. My fingers were
black with atrociously regular poems that reverted to
oblivion over their syllables, as woodlice in chainmail,
torsos raised, file together toward their damp-soled
sentines. I loved neighborhoods as we love mistresses. The years might have thrown me into the hustle
and bustle of trades, of destinies, of distresses and
prudences, of swells and gatherings, I rolled around
in life with a head in estrus, with a happiness in my
shoulders the memory of which today brings me to
tears. My entire presence is wrapped around this
glorious past, like a vine of hops around a garden
gate. Ah! how I would like to see myself, painless and
hurried, in those streets that the dead have carried
among the dead! Often, my daily head wavers under
the pulsions of the images of my inner library: the
shadow of my mother at the top of the staircase in
the Faubourg Saint-Martin, the Sunday friends who
brought me gifts of fried food in my room, gallops

of Percherons from under the nave of the métro, the brewers' apron with its colors of an old commode, the newspaper vendor, whom a gust of wind transformed into an Indian chief, the jerry can of the soldier on leave from which one saw the blood of Verdun dripping, the police officers who had time, between two cows as tall as armoires, to caress the Limousin goats passing through Paris. What fine tinkling in the soul!

Then, the rain of hyperboles moistened the Old World. Then came the great problems, the high questions, the tidal waves of philosophy, realist politics, exophthalmic individualism, Cartesian racism, scientific materialism, lichenean criticism, Communist art, endocrinian mysticism, symbolic polygamies, ideas that we had nevertheless surpassed 30 years earlier ... The Army invaded the displays of booksellers and was transformed into novels, treaties, manifestoes. A year passed, and this mobilization was replaced with another. I pity those who were forced to write about cars, about aviation, about communism. What repetitions, what poverty, what errors! They didn't even cheat. No poet has had the coquetry or the audacity to invent an imaginary film, an eccentric politics, or volatile art. Everyone believed in the thing and entered into poncifs the way one settles into a villa. Paris began to flow with theories. They barely let you live. We had to sniff at close range the black prick of war to form the fasces ...

I don't know if I have lived, I don't know if I have dreamed. But I found myself, one day, in the middle of the Parisian sea as the principal concierge of the Chêne de Charles II must have seen it through his lyre-shaped lorgnette. I was surrounded by geniuses. There was the genius of dramatic art, that of political economy, that of the newspaper for single ladies, that of the fireplaces of salons, that of the spirit of the Army of Peace, that of French Thought, and that of the Goutte de Lait. Madame de Haute-Toidelat, her stretch marks rising up to her eyes, but she boasted of recognizing the pianists just by the way they hailed a taxi. Monsieur d'Empressé presided over the Club of Rediscovered Human Consciousness. We made cocktails with bouillon eyes, Gruyère holes, and *vin de l'assassin*. We were in a room where some jackanapes had organized an Exhibition, the object of which was to oblige the visitors to commit hara-kiri out of admiration. On the walls: the suspenders of a poet, with the inscription: a poet's suspenders; well-preserved calluses, with the notice: partridge-eye of a painter's right foot; the single hair of a mustache, accompanied by a few words: hair from the mustache of a corporal of the 6th engineers; a photograph: the legs of 1938 Parisiennes; a Celtic cigarette, which was said to be: a cigarette smoked by a Frenchman; a frying pan, with its instructions: a pan in which men brown their onions, escalope, ideas, and other foodstuffs. And so on for kilometers. Science, the World, Official Art and Garage Art, magistracy and intelligence, swooning sensitivity and politeness. Out of that event some collectors took away a few mustache hairs and a few grains of tobacco. The next day, the papers gave an account of the affair and were lost in transcendent commentaries on the state of perfection of Civilization, on the originality of the organizers, etc.

Of course, I had dreamed, good people, but I had dreamed, I believe, on the side of the righteous. So accurately that my ear perceived the murmur of the people: agriculture lacks hands, the repopulation lacks kidneys, the Basses-Alpes lacks citizens, aviation lacks pilots, French craftsmen lack simple and diligent French. Then, the demon that presides over the neomenias of the City of Light turned the page. A well-meaning deputy, who arched himself in the rostrum like a seahorse sucking on a swazzle, made a speech on the necessity of voting the Week of the Fourth Thursday in order to enable the citizens of the Republic to read, learn, and meditate. Days passed. And we all found ourselves, intellectuals, politicians, salon escapees, young poets with feverish gums, fashion ambassadors, fascists, Conservators of Garters and congested snobs, survivors of the Great Fear, personalities representative of France at work, of France in bed, of France in the cottage, of France in lace, of France at the ballot box, of France in general dress rehearsals, we all found ourselves before the manger of a level crossing blocked by burning trains ...

All this, it's an invasion of ants. Kill one, millions of new ones return. I returned to my sad and faithful room where my old suits were greeted, sleeves raised, wrists outstretched. The pants walked with a goose step, the gas mask turned in the middle of the room like a German top. Life is a myth. My soul and myself, we packed our bags and sought lodging in the neighborhood. Bread is simple, love is simple, death is simple. Why did the poor men want life so complicated? Why do they stuff it with the envy of their fantasies? What fatigue, and what waste! Prisons, we need prisons for all these usurpers. They invite us into their theaters to listen to the dialogues of bra vendors, or into their parliaments to hear the harangues of village drummers, or into their salons to admire the Venus Teinturière. Live! Doctor, I would like to live! Why aren't men like the leaves of a tree, all clean, silent, and discreet? Must there be elite souls? Yes, well, there must. And the brains of princes and the sensitivities of great men. Yes, but you don't just need those. Paris must have above all regular people and not geniuses on every floor, like dentists or tailors. I am not a partisan, I said, I am not a militiaman, hardly a poet. I am just a man who watches from his lighthouse, a bee that carries his black honey on his back, a passerby among passersby.

I love life, as mole crickets love their path, and the tiles stand shoulder to shoulder on the temples of houses. I would like to do my duty as a man among real shows, "in rich banality." I wish there was a lighthouse only every thousand meters on this road that leads us to death. Geniuses, but men. No, I am not a theologian, nor a fascist, nor a red, nor a mauve, nor a unionist, nor one of the most brilliant novelists of this time, nor the most prominent dramatist, nor the most active traveling clerk of French Thought, nor one of the most adorable Pontiffs of Letters, nor a charming conversationalist, nor an ornament of the salons. I am only a lamp of flesh and of shadow. Yet I sense what is good and what is false. I attached my existence to the hearse of the poor. And I prefer to bite into the sausage of Mother Bourdognon than to take it seriously. All these geniuses frighten me. What if they had at least brought joys, if they had created something? Because, finally, there was Rabelais, Balzac, Pascal, Baudelaire, Stendhal, Musset, Father Hugo, that great lender whose name they all keep silent. There was Rimbaud, Mallarmé, Verlaine, and Debussy. Likewise, there were Bizet and Fragonard. And all of those before them. So, don't shake up the good people in their beds because young Fartproof has given birth to a foulio, a playlet, a bland ditty, a brief trifle, or an outmoded painting. Otherwise, we're going to call the artillerymen to their pieces in our turn, we who have a hundred years and more of the corners of Paris, and of books, and of diligence. Us too, we have a Revolution that threatens behind our fagots. But an obscure, dignified revolution, full of fantastic vigils, of good-natured desires. A whim of Poetry, a more artistic declaration of love for the material. An authorization given to men to risk themselves entirely, body and soul, in the adventure! It would take a Revolution of courage against ease, of meditation against glibness, of true art against the art within everyone's reach. And, from my chamber of silence and of lassitude, I see them coming, those who will do it, in the name of the honor of feeling.

Danse Mabraque

… And indeed, we were among men. Ah! there weren't many left. Laos, Gironde, Peru, Spanish Morocco had collapsed. It took ten hours to go from Place du Palais Bourbon to Bourg-la-Reine, six days to get to Saint-Pierre-des-Corps. Alps of warm bitumen had risen between the great centers of Europe. The first colors of the afterlife landscapes appeared at the crossroads. Stretches of rails, sometimes reaching as high as one thousand feet and reminiscent of the arborescent ferns of the youth of the world, jutted out of the ground, topped by a locomotive that creaked and swayed at their top, like a pair of suspenders, once upon a time, at the skylight of an old town roof. Borborygmic ballistics rose to the chapped lips of the craters. One of the first, I leant my ear to it.

My grandmother used to say that if the stomach could speak, it would whisper in a plaintive voice: "Carrots, carrots …" The world that was collapsing, like a huge soufflé, could certainly not speak either. But we nonetheless heard it shrieking through all the fissures of the catastrophe: "I love you … I love you, I love you …" It was not flesh that swallowed it, nor vertebrae, nor even terrestrial crowds that the planets, placed in the first rank, recognized by their overcoats, but feelings. We were dying through our hearts. We were distraught with anguish at the slide toward nothingness, as if we had to abandon forever our loved ones. And nothing remained for men of their machines, their telegraphs, their speeds, their manometers, their films, their politics, nothing remained for them of what was illusory, of what we had all taken for strength, for power. We had only our love on our backs and before our eyes. And we learned at last that love was the only thing that had given us a bit of brilliance, a little pause, a little time.

A unique temperature had descended on us from the dull heavens, initialed by the drifting trees that hastened toward other laws. Bluish temperature, which forced some to cover themselves with furs or papers, others to wander naked … The dogs stuck out their tongues, but the fish burst like frozen sacks, stiff at the bottom of rivers that emptied like bathtubs, and the water went through holes toward obscure larynxes. The door handles were covered with frost, as wasp-riddled fruit fell like marmalade amidst the squamous and leprous sidewalks. Climates, winds, and odors were mixed up like the colors of a palette: asparagus could be seen growing in bookstores; lemon trees were blooming in a cluster of trams; mollusks were found where there had been calves' heads, emeralds, or umbrellas. The facades of the buildings were still standing, almost all of them, but painted with fire, covered with snails, scoria, human eyes. It seemed as if ink had flowed from the upper floors to the basements, that the liquid of the sky had fallen quite otherwise than in the form of rain on the reliefs of a world in perdition. There were pink puddles, the pure pink of a molting maiden, green ponds, a beautiful green carpet, sleeping in a province. A river of glue was coming and going in Paris, at the speed of a bus, carrying birds, cigarettes, and gaping pianos that opened to reveal the skeletons of gazelles. We knew nothing. We heard nothing. The din was so powerful and so new that it reached the mysterious immensity of silence.

Sometimes a man would approach you and shout:

— Is it you?

— Yes, me, you replied.

— My God! The bus conductors were transformed into Easter eggs last night! Tomorrow, it will be the pedicures' turn, then the postmen, the opticians, the leatherworkers, the scientists, the nobles, the ziblocousses, the cacotermes, the pantagreels, and the botonglouzes.

— But there are no more tomorrows, no more nights, no more days, no more rhythms ...

— It's true, there's nothing left ... Goodbye. Come tomorrow anyway, sir, we will try to find our neighborhoods, we will dine together ...

— Are you Parisian, too?

— No, I'm from Toul ... But I just saw the streets of Toul, there, behind this huge horse ... I saw them, as we see children on the arms of mothers in Italian paintings. Goodbye, beautiful blond ... Luterdu pourquil aholoé! ...

And the man suddenly disappeared. He was bursting under your nose like a light bulb. And there was nothing left of him but a short, comical smoke, such as the red whip that once signaled the disappearance of Mephistopheles on the stage of the Amboise Theater, or that of Charleville.

Nevertheless, I had found it, me, my neighborhood. My real neighborhood, the only one, that one of the Gare de l'Est. The others, subsequently, they were just dresses on this skeleton. That is, I had found only a fragment of it in the middle of a jewelry store in ruins. The métro had fled toward Saturn, like a rosary of champagne corks, when the Earth had ceased spinning. The butchers' shops of Rue d'Aubervilliers, decorated with peonies and carnations since the earliest times, swam in a paradisiac soup out of which flew royal blue cannons, light as dragonflies. I entered a swimming pool that served as a meeting place for those whom chance alone kept in the same spot on mad earth. Because we could find ourselves perfectly, without the slightest sensation of change, from one moment to the next, on a viaduct, in Parma, in Chaillac, in Melbourne, in Vancouver, on the edge of a precipice, in a salon, on a steamship. We were still invisible to other living beings, but as enormous as centuries. We were the microbes in a drop of water, the grains in a kilo of rice, the hairs in a lord-mayor's wig. In the anthills too there are cathedrals, mornings, words, Sundays, family lives, dramas, passions, military journals. But do we see them? A wagon wheel, and that's the end of this civilization. And so with us. All the patience, all the prudence, all the worldly, banking, or sporting combinations of our world had offered no more resistance than a revolution of cockchafers. Within hours, the capitals had melted like butter in a pan. It was neither the typhoon, nor the monsoon, nor the lava flow, but a change of scenery that still valiant imaginations connected to some general strike, to some day after Pentecost or some wildly hot day in August. It reminded you of old failures, of cities troubled by a political event, or by the threat of war. But these physiognomies of the past filled us with regrets. Because they were nothing compared to the colossal landslide that folded the planet's bed like a wallet ...

Thus, I entered the pool. There a hurricane had heaped cars, pylons, post offices, and the bric-à-brac of shops. An odor of general mobilization hung over the chaos. Men stood in groups in the midst of this disorder and looked at one another. None of them had a memory. The eyes were opaque and sad like gumballs. Useless hands hung from bodies. They were there, the men of my neighborhood, the bistro owner, the glazier, the cobbler, the peddler, the renter, the beggar. I recognized them. But they, forgetful, united in stupefaction, no longer had any memory of me. Already, they were the sugar in a cup of tea. They were ending the lives of many millions of people. Pell-mell, their feet in their mouths, they were leaning against the doorstop. And I, who still possessed gestures, inflections, who walked with a heavy and precise foot on still warm ground, I begged them to welcome me into their oblivion. Happy men, they were already part of the final hour. And me, I was still drawing my past, I was looking everywhere for dear shadows, I waited for moving voices, I was running after silhouettes. There remained in my soul the prolongations of friendship, a need for violent and well-known words. What had become, in the turmoil, of those talkative hairdressers, those subtle pharmacists, those welcoming restaurateurs who had helped me to live through the time I was poor, abandoned, unhappy? For I had been unhappy and oppressed, for I had been hunted down and cautious in the days when the happiness of men slapped like a flag on a torpedo boat. I had been bullied by opulence, martyred by lazy stupidity, trampled by château prostitutes, snubbed by bad chamber music, splattered by the despicable dandies of the theater. And now that the same men, instead of experiencing misfortune in their turn, were sinking into comfortable luxuries that perpetuated their stupid luxury, I continued, me, to push with a robust and serious knee the barrel of black misfortune. I felt eternal in the midst of this mud-stained, gold-drenched world that ended like a New Year's Eve. I was going toward the end of everything like a shocking echo destined never to die.

And how sad it was to walk on and encounter the utmost end without finding anything of what I had loved or hated! I was lost in a forest of strange noctilucas, in a helpless city that hovered like a hawk over the stampede. I recognized everything and I recognized nothing. My soul had moved forward and made zigzags, like a dog happy not to feel the kennel behind it. The grass, the metaphors, the blue mice, the anger, the pebbles burning like wildfire. We saw the numbers on our heads, the grammatical rules, the first names, the insults fleeing and diluting in the air, like colonies of Argonauts. A sort of clawed autumn, glittering with sun-animals, everything torn apart, everything denuded. The aspirators of Astral Mythology swallowed up matter *&* spirit. And our eyes saw it, our ears heard it!

— Our ears, our eyes, our sensibilities … peuh! said the old Hermaphrodite Conservative who clung to me, peuh! shells, shards, peelings, nothing, swaddling clothes, of spoilt children, limpets, spon-dyles, calptrates, scaly oscarbins! Squadrons of 3, of 9, of Anne-Marie, of the Rhône, of +, of % were flying above us. Pauls whirled around, mixing with Charleses, lice, cabbages, knees, pebbles, owls. The ether was hunchbacked, for the matter of the World was overflowing with its perfect and supposed form. It was no longer an orange or a rod of rushes in the sideboards, as we were told in the olden days, but a stained-glass window of caramels that merged with the entrails of men clumped together with tooth-brushes, with the washrooms of butterflies. Beards were growing everywhere during these months of debacle. But to think of finding a hairdresser, a knife, the lid of a can of peas, was like wanting to die of stupidity. My cheeks were covered with scales of sole skin. But, oddly enough, I didn't want to scratch myself. The itching had left us like the hunger. It was noteworthy indeed: none of us were hungry. And since the demon is everywhere, even at the height of the Apocalypse, when we no longer needed him, we would spot restaurants! There were no more doormen, no more glass, no more matches, no more diseases, no more soap. But there were still restaurants, as strange in their blinding solitude as fringes of snow, formerly, in the middle of an already cheerful meadow, in the middle of April. April, I said to myself, it's true. March, April, May, June, Gex, Nantua, Belley, Trévoux. The eye was in the tomb and looked at Cain, Opéra, Quatre-Septembre, Bourse, Sentier, Louis XIV, Louis XV, Louis XVI ... My, Your, His, I put down 7 and I remember 2!

It's right. Better to die like an army of candles. To have had the world, to have possessed gold, eye, sperm, finger, to come up with such nonsense, it's really too much. That's all we found: adultery, cocktail, pimp, Jewish finance, brothel, copyright, the *sou* of the franc, the rule of three. And those dog-nosed lovers who can't be bothered to work miracles! Let us resign ourselves to clamoring without insolence, without backfiring. Let us hold our places on the luminous toboggan, as hot and paternal as a suburban locomotive. Let us slide into the supreme dust of the sooty factory. If we serve to constitute another world, and we are toes, jacket sleeves, or corkscrews in a finer, more durable civilization than ours, we will still consider ourselves happy. But this one is done for. Come on, shoo, we're closing, take a look behind the wings!

The women were the first to be swallowed up. They had fled like a boarding school. The old and the ugly were rotting on the spot, like lettuce. But in Paris, which trembled like a tooth, you could no longer find a hairdresser, a stick of rouge, a Pekinese, or a pair of Louis XV heels. They had carried away their wings and their lies. And everything was unraveling down there, far away in the void, like a knot of smoke. Nothing. Nothing remained of what had sustained, for years, the faltering gaze and forced marches. Not a knee that could be glimpsed, not a crimped eye, not a wet lip, not a bloody fingernail, not a thigh as soft as a jackboot. The boat had thrown them first, all our mistresses, into the torrential Sabbath, a thousand leagues from ideas and brains. And not a single piece of information remained. It was the poets alone who, at times, could explain the fall of the curtain on the final stew. There were no more newspapers and no more wheels, no more sharp instruments and no more watches, no more mirrors and no more stairs. Men walked sometimes without nerves and some-times without ears. They walked and they stopped: a huge hole cynically widened & they rushed into it.

But I knew they would never hit bottom, because there was no bottom. The fall of men became the dust of men. And this dust itself, suddenly vertiginous, reached without transition the highest degree of the imponderable.

And I saw that everything was becoming nothing. The newspaper kiosk became paper, and from paper it turned into tracing paper. The rivers rose from the ground like ribbons of sticky paper. The roofs of the train stations were breaking apart, revealing spongy trains reduced to the state of caterpillars. Hundred-year-old vagabonds, clinging to the remains of the planet by the antiquity of their errands, sometimes went without shoulders, sometimes without heads. Only the legs held strong. But the world was still shrinking...

Often, the questions of the mediocre razed the facades like whispers. The last thoughts of those who had no more understood Nothingness than the Infinite. Nothing to do. So-and-so wanted to know how the radio, the music-hall, syndicalism, diplomacy, Esperanto, the Stock Exchange, circles and barracks had ended. Another was trying to save ideas, principles, laws. Sometimes, the lamentations died down. We could no longer hear the seas unite in a wrestling of green bitumen and the volcanoes blending their Jupiterian voices. There was no more weather, nuances, or forecasts. Day lasted eight seconds & gave way to winter in one minute. Several springs were springing up at the same time, and one could see pink roses by the millions galloping on a patch of ground quivering with stars. Then, summer dawned, mingled with moons and hair. The angels were fleeing. We could feel them sometimes, white and icy jostling between our elbows. And, always, the world was shrinking! My senses told me that there were no more Poles, no more America, no more Japan, no more Scandinavia. The Earth was neither flat nor round. We were the last to guess it, we the last, only as a strip of sand under our feet. No doubt, there were still hectares and hectares. But the end was drawing near as a station darts off to meet an express train. As we passed from moment to moment, we saw the disappearance of birds, grass, chimneys, horses, water, clouds, shadows. It was neither night nor day, neither hot nor cold. I was nothing more than weight in the middle of a landscape both industrial and Saharan where the details of what had been the glittering and cluttered world were seen at intervals: a revolver, a tin of tuna in oil, a comb, a boat, an ax, an inkwell, a tuxedo. Thus, during the war of 1914, during the war in China, during the Spanish Civil War, and during the ensuing wars, soldiers sometimes entered a bombed-out house and found, among the shards of flesh and heaps of plaster, an intact copy of the waltzes of Chopin, near a small glass filled to the brim with Green Chartreuse ...

Soon, there was nothing before the last men but a long boulevard beyond which the Void could be read like a poster. The Earth Affair was liquidated. It died like a Love. It is mistakenly believed that women will never leave you. What a joke: they are handfuls of water, pastilles on a tongue. They evaporate like ether. They disappear like a serious Reblochon between the knives of real connoisseurs. We had thought the Earth to be indestructible and welded to autogenous matter. It had been covered with rails, nightclubs, seaports, embassies, beet fields. It had been weighed down with masquerades, wars, air raids. We had stuffed it with snobs, like a good turkey. In short, what was said was done. We had settled down as friends on the steps of this solid staircase. We were there, what, we were counting, we were getting by. There was even love for the poor. And now everything flowed over the marmite! This Europe, this Asia that is losing its hair like skulls, eh! Imagine reading a book, the Railway Guide, for example, and suddenly you see the characters disappear before your eyes. The pages go blank. Then those pages flee in their turn. And soon there is no more table, no more chair under your buttocks. You feel that it's your turn next. This is how the machine jammed and finally let us go. What had been the Universe of Hindus, Chinese, Egyptians, Greeks & Romans, the universe of Napoleon, that of Freemasonry, of International Boxing

Federations, the universe of Western Union, of Air France, the universe of Marlène Dietrich, of Poincaré, of Mustapha Kemal, the universe of sugars and of dollars, of Meunier Chocolate, Dunlop tires, Pernod fils, my world and yours, that of the manicure and that of La Païva, that of the clowns and that of the chromosomes, it's nothing more than an alley, mille-feuilles, a footbridge, a pencil line. The universe was frying like an andouille. A few moments later, and I will no longer see these vestiges of profusion that decorate our agony like splendid detritus: a Titian, a box of caviar from Petrossian, a bottle of Juliénas, a Swiss army knife, a pagoda, village roofs, a silver fox, a hornbill with its beak like a tank, a locomotive, a stabbed dove, a pair of espadrilles, a bike and a pen. Something else, no doubt, but I can no longer see it … There are half a dozen of us, like returning from an expedition: a priest (because there is always a priest), a long-term captain, a Spaniard from the ruined army, two strangers and myself. We lack our voice, and we are too disgusted to make gestures. We are unhappy. It's the end. I think that the first principle of any phenomenon, which must be god some place or other, has doubtless willed that the consciousness of world's end should be collected by six good men. I'm one of them. And we are the bottom of the pot. Thus, the day after a gala, we find, on the benches of the Café de Paris, the dust, the husks, the dandruff, and the bark of an organized city. Where there had been princesses, all that remains are sweat stains ...

The world was dying in the form of a cloud in the churning immensity of emptiness and clarity. One of those loving green clouds that persist in the sky, like long lianas, like arms, like languor, while, long ago, the sun has fallen like an egg yolk deep into the radiant navel of the sea.

Again ...

Again! That idiot alarm clock just tore through my room like an explosive bullet. It senses, it is there, it settles down. I still have at least 115 dormant kilograms. And yet I feel it, my mouth is full. A very hot thought still coming from behind me murmurs astonished, in a goitrous voice: "Huh? What? What is this? Who? Monday? Tuesday? Huh? He rang? What does he want? Give me a break! There's a fire? What, answer! ..."

But there's no doubt! We are remade, my death and myself. He's there, and he hasn't changed his suit, and he hasn't wiped his feet. It's him, during the day, with his clip-on tie, his stupid colonial eye, his housekeeper face, a pawn, adjutant, morning hen, deceptive lover. Good gods! Yet I had closed the doors last night, and the windows and faucets, and the boxes and books. I had hid myself in my pains. I had given instructions to my migraine, to my liver, to the electric button. Vaguely, I'd given myself the gift of a citadel. He entered anyway, the brute! He would pass through the eye of a needle; he would find cracks, wounds, crevices, waxy nests, pores, atom holes through which to invade me, like volcanic dust.

And there it is, stretching out above me, breath thinning; there it is weighing me, hopping, with great scaffolding gestures, broadcast references, rigging coquetries, dirty contortions of factory smoke. Ah! yes, it has a bad face! It could have left me on the brink of life until midday. But no, it chose me among a thousand, poor sleeper, it won me from the lottery, and it's targeting me. I would like to throw myself back, to dive back in, to find that corner where the tide of sleep has not yet withdrawn. But the bed is a false witness. I hear it beating me down, leaving me all alone at this time when you have to think about life all at once, as a whole. It gives me the impression of swallowing a pill, one of those military hospital pills that serve equally well for man and horse, the Frenchman and the Enemy. Funny taste. And it doesn't pass, the bitch. In vain do I brace myself, arm myself, seek out the weak point, rely on gambling tricks, and quickly tell myself: "This one will lend me a hundred thousand francs; I will say that I was sick; for the tax bill, no hurry ... From there I'll return on foot ... I'll have lunch in a taxi ..." — I'm good ... This day looks like gelatin, with the resistances of kidneys that make me feel around for a cudgel. A day that could teach me how to tap into life!

And now it wants to play the mother of a family. I'm given five minutes of respite. You'll pay in monthly installments, but you will still pay, and far more. I go down a few steps, I find my way into sleep again. Sleep, sleep ... I see it, the color of an evening

dress, with its black cheeks, its bitter teeth, its espadrilles, in a cloud all sonorous with soap bubbles, all
vaporous with oil. A gendarme's fist puts handcuffs
around my ears. And Life begins to fall again like
rain, to search like a flashlight for discarded pants,
and whose ... suspenders hang, like intestines; on
the café au lait, which wrinkles like an old woman's
breast; on the registered letter from the telegraph
office; on Whosits novel, which has the complexion
of Gruyère, just like Whosists himself. I watch out
for it, too, me, and I wait for the moment when it
bends down to look under the bed, like a cuckold. It
only takes a moment, and I slip it between her empty
parentheses! Nothing to do. It dabs me, dries my lazy
places, like a chatterbox. It drinks me, auscultates me;
it realizes that I have neither a cold, nor cancer, nor
a fractured fibula. Go, out! Fit for work.

I say no with everything I have. I cling to the train
of the drapes. I take the big hand of the quilt. I don't
care! It's there, holding me, forcing me to act like a
raped woman, to sweat like a death row inmate, with
the spasms of one serving time. And what fingernails,
what depth of throat, what a close-up of a gardener!
I risk a little hypocritical movement, a real pretense
of being wounded. I begin to see myself at home. Ah!
it seems heavy, this telephone like the head of an
astonished black man, with its automatic teeth. And
the door queasy with its vertigo of 20 years! And this

floorboard, as quick to scream as a dog's tail under a man's foot! Everything bothers me, pisses me off, mocks me, gives me trouble. Grain stores that don't want to open up, tire warehouses, river bellies, my eyelids, my poor heavy eyelids, my poor homeless eyelids, sans family, indebted and perspicacious, the eyelids of a fattened monk, municipal see-saw and adultery, my airplane-canvas tinted eyelids try to repel with light movements this stupid hairy Morning, this big moron, this street calfskin lamppost that is there to grimace, to sit on my chairs, to heckle my navel, to start me off with a short cut of tobacco, the sour smell of a pipe, the shamed step, its trams, its Gares de l'Est, whose packs jeer behind my back!

Already the newspapers are printed in the slightest folds made by my surprised and ruminating face. Memories erupt in fours. Ideas cough and greet each other while descending the stairs of my condyles, like civil servants. My anxiety, always ready at the start, is already waiting for me at the little bar, bayonet fixed. Come on, answer NOW! Hypocrisy? *Present*. Ambition? *Present*. Hunger? *Present!* Gold filling? *Present*. Nothing to report? No sick people? Okay, so let's go! And here I am again for a quarter of a second, all alone, with a life that mocks me, and which evolves, and which revels, and which yells in the street. Sarabandes, banners, rollmops, mopsias, seraphim ... But what do they want from me? Castanets of birds dart past my window, in a hurry to catch another round trip on the Dauphine-Nation line. Milkmen piss, newspaper in hand. The meat rises from the Halles like a riot. My knee is ready, my hands impatient, my ribs have nothing against it setting forth. No more mistakes! These ant-hill noises, these tree-wheels, these cataracts of sinks, which are spit from one arrondissement to another, this kitchenware harnessed by concierges, all that, it's morning, it's Paris, that's the refrain. Itchy hair and ringing doorbells that penetrate the skin of my apartment like syringes. I take a big step toward things. I no longer have an ocean in my head, no more tunnels in my limbs, no more parachutes in my guts. Yes, what, I can't sleep anymore! I know you. No matter how many times you call yourself Monday the 18th or Tuesday the 23rd, you won't get me today. Hey! Ah! you're still the same, with your inventors of checks, of tax stamps, of your rich people's trash, your toad budgets, your winter sports anthrax. Come on, I'm your man.

It begins to dominate me, because I'm still quite weak and stuffed; I'm still all marrow and eraser. And I feel like a Goliath in the sand of my bed. Tied up, half-spoiled, half-devastated. I'm gently chained, while the Parisian morning whispers horrors to me in a harelip voice. A marriage rests on my stomach like a paperweight. The tailor's bill drives a big stake into my right knee. A woman I caught a glimpse of yesterday wraps herself gently around my left knee. My age pinches my calves. The lack of coal runs through my head like a giant scarab. The nomination of Rumpless at the Museum of Goldfish stings me in the heel. The work to be done rises to my chest. And decisions come down, as in Gravelotte! The feeling that it will rain sprinkles me with drops of ink. Hope runs her guns along the nape of my neck and thus avoids disgust, crouching before my nostrils like a pretentious mastiff.

The alarm clock pedals on my big track. Fatigues bristle up, but I, still in pain, drive them back like onlookers. I would really like to die innocently during the years that I am going to put into my training, leaning on my palms, stepping free of the tons of sugar melting down my thighs. I wish I could no longer see myself stretched out, unrolled, covered in beams and rubble. Have I time to want? Have I said that I wanted to? I said nothing. I arose like a vapor. I was shot at point blank range by a large fog cannon. And I hear the shaving brush, the collar button, the comb with its disheveled eyelashes, the toothbrush, the mirrored armoire all crying out for a miracle. Life bows down. I did things well. Life gives way. I let it freeze around me as if I were bathing.

The neighborhood radios run after me, whistling gymnastics for idlers, wheat and mutton rates, ministerial dinners, pharmaceutical hymns, smoked goods at so much a bundle. The smell of proverbs swirls in the street. Here is a sky the color of eggnog that bores itself watching Paris live. My bed remains open like a lexicon where all the now useless dreams are arranged by verbs and pronouns, all my hollows, all the folds that my body has embroidered while sleeping. Standing, I take down my shadow, I palpate the void, I try a gesture, like playing number 13. To see. The propeller is turning. The cogs are rusty but obedient. I'm leaving the day aside for now; it will not go to waste. We'll talk about it again. I'll take it sideways. Meanwhile, my mind has come to the end of this travail of an iconoclastic fly. It breaks the pale, restless shell in which my fungus form was enclosed, as if constructed of fragile drugs, and as fatigued as a salad. I don't have, Me, any of those awakenings of fencers, gangsters, bumpkins, or seagulls that are always ready to slay worldly, athletic, or industrial existence, with idea-dictaphones, mechanical brooms, and brains from Rue de la Paix. My life is a good and brave life at so much per minute, and one that knows it in the corners, with its fresh virgin wallet in its pistol pocket. Not so dumb.

It got me, this morning, like a landlady. But we will meet tonight, face to face, when I force it to wear out along the sad streets of factories, before monkey-bottomed bistros, around the buses with seborrhea, at the back of squares all vibrating with cockroaches. When the earrings of the old leucorrhoeic houses sparkle, when the nipples of the night shoot, in the traffic jams of men, false news, sighs, when I finally walk my valiant bones, awake like a ghost, in random neighborhoods the color of guinea fowl and watering cans, when my body of a Western sleeper is cooked for revenge, it will be my turn, I'll get back at it, Life!

Acknowledgements

To translate Léon-Paul Fargue is considerably challenging, akin perhaps to engaging in a kind of acrobatic act which, aside from being bold, is to some degree even perilous. If you don't think so, well, *in the beginning was the word...* These things can give birth to worlds, even if one doesn't believe in spectres. The task was to let Fargue manifest and take possession of me and arise anew in the mask of English. If I appear anywhere, *tant pis* for this slippage.

At the end of this shamanic high wire act, I was aided by the better eyes of a few companions, including Gregory Flanders, Pierre Joris, and, at the final hour, Pierre Senges, whose acumen clarified a few Rabelasian, quasi-surrealist, Jabberwockian passages. I am grateful to each of them, but it is to Peter Thompson to whom I owe the greatest debt, for his precise, thorough, and extensive observations, sometimes down to the most atomic of details. Although I fell from the rope a number of times, this translation is infinitely superior due to their eyes.

To close, I wish to extend my gratitude to Robert & Olivia Temple and The Montparnasse Cultural Foundation for their support, as well as for the even greater gift of their unparalleled patience. At last, the fated moment for this aperitif, *truite au bleu*, and so much more, has arrived. Before it, may you be like *l'homme foudroyé*.

COLOPHON

HIGH SOLITUDE
was handset in InDesign CC.

The text font is *JAF Lapture*.

The display font is *Curve*.

Book design & typesetting: Alessandro Segalini

Cover design: CMP

Image credit: Jacques Callot & Melchior Tavernier,
*Le plan de la ville, cité université, fauxbourgs de Paris,
avec la description de son antiquité* (1630).

HIGH SOLITUDE
is published by Contra Mundum Press.

Contra Mundum Press   New York · London · Melbourne

CONTRA MUNDUM PRESS

Dedicated to the value & the indispensable importance of the individual voice, to works that test the boundaries of thought & experience.

The primary aim of Contra Mundum is to publish translations of writers who in their use of form and style are *à rebours*, or who deviate significantly from more programmatic & spurious forms of experimentation. Such writing attests to the volatile nature of modernism. Our preference is for works that have not yet been translated into English, are out of print, or are poorly translated, for writers whose thinking & æsthetics are in opposition to timely or mainstream currents of thought, value systems, or moralities. We also reprint obscure and out-of-print works we consider significant but which have been forgotten, neglected, or overshadowed.

There are many works of fundamental significance to *Weltliteratur* (& *Weltkultur*) that still remain in relative oblivion, works that alter and disrupt standard circuits of thought — these warrant being encountered by the world at large. It is our aim to render them more visible.

For the complete list of forthcoming publications, please visit our website. To be added to our mailing list, send your name and email address to: info@contramundum.net

Contra Mundum Press
P.O. Box 1326
New York, NY 10276
USA

2012   *Gilgamesh*
        Ghérasim Luca, *Self-Shadowing Prey*
        Rainer J. Hanshe, *The Abdication*
        Walter Jackson Bate, *Negative Capability*
        Miklós Szentkuthy, *Marginalia on Casanova*
        Fernando Pessoa, *Philosophical Essays*
2013   Elio Petri, *Writings on Cinema & Life*
        Friedrich Nietzsche, *The Greek Music Drama*
        Richard Foreman, *Plays with Films*
        Louis-Auguste Blanqui, *Eternity by the Stars*
        Miklós Szentkuthy, *Towards the One & Only Metaphor*
        Josef Winkler, *When the Time Comes*
2014   William Wordsworth, *Fragments*
        Josef Winkler, *Natura Morta*
        Fernando Pessoa, *The Transformation Book*
        Emilio Villa, *The Selected Poetry of Emilio Villa*
        Robert Kelly, *A Voice Full of Cities*
        Pier Paolo Pasolini, *The Divine Mimesis*
        Miklós Szentkuthy, *Prae, Vol. 1*
2015   Federico Fellini, *Making a Film*
        Robert Musil, *Thought Flights*
        Sándor Tar, *Our Street*
        Lorand Gaspar, *Earth Absolute*
        Josef Winkler, *The Graveyard of Bitter Oranges*
        Ferit Edgü, *Noone*
        Jean-Jacques Rousseau, *Narcissus*
        Ahmad Shamlu, *Born Upon the Dark Spear*
2016   Jean-Luc Godard, *Phrases*
        Otto Dix, *Letters, Vol. 1*
        Maura Del Serra, *Ladder of Oaths*
        Pierre Senges, *The Major Refutation*
        Charles Baudelaire, *My Heart Laid Bare & Other Texts*
2017   Joseph Kessel, *Army of Shadows*
        Rainer J. Hanshe & Federico Gori, *Shattering the Muses*
        Gérard Depardieu, *Innocent*
        Claude Mouchard, *Entangled — Papers! — Notes*

2018   Miklós Szentkuthy, *Black Renaissance*
       Adonis & Pierre Joris, *Conversations in the Pyrenees*
2019   Charles Baudelaire, *Belgium Stripped Bare*
       Robert Musil, *Unions*
       Iceberg Slim, *Night Train to Sugar Hill*
       Marquis de Sade, *Aline & Valcour*
2020   *A City Full of Voices: Essays on the Work of Robert Kelly*
       Rédoine Faïd, *Outlaw*
       Carmelo Bene, *I Appeared to the Madonna*
       Paul Celan, *Microliths They Are, Little Stones*
       Zsuzsa Selyem, *It's Raining in Moscow*
       Bérengère Viennot, *Trumpspeak*
       Robert Musil, *Theater Symptoms*
       Miklós Szentkuthy, *Chapter on Love*
2021   Charles Baudelaire, *Paris Spleen*
       Marguerite Duras, *The Darkroom*
       Andrew Dickos, *Honor Among Thieves*
       Pierre Senges, *Ahab (Sequels)*
       Carmelo Bene, *Our Lady of the Turks*
2022   Fernando Pessoa, *Writings on Art & Poetical Theory*
       Miklós Szentkuthy, *Prae, Vol. 2*
       Blixa Bargeld, *Europe Crosswise: A Litany*
       Pierre Joris, *Always the Many, Never the One*
       Robert Musil, *Literature & Politics*
2023   Pierre Joris, *Interglacial Narrows*
       Gabriele Tinti, *Bleedings — Incipit Tragœdia*
       Évelyne Grossman, *The Creativity of the Crisis*
       Rainer J. Hanshe, *Closing Melodies*
       Kari Hukkila, *One Thousand & One*
2024   Antonin Artaud, *Journey to Mexico*
       Rainer J. Hanshe, *Dionysos Speed*
       Amina Saïd, *Walking the Earth*

SOME FORTHCOMING TITLES

Nuriá Perpinyà, *And, Suddenly, Paradise*
Marquis de Sade, *Stories, Tales, & Fables*

AGRODOLCE SERIES ÆD

2020   Dejan Lukić, *The Oyster*
2022   Ugo Tognazzi, *The Injester*

HY**PERION**
On the Future of Æsthetics   2006–PRESENT

To read samples and order current & back issues of *Hyperion*,
visit contramundumpress.com/hyperion
Edited by Rainer J. Hanshe & Erika Mihálycsa (2014 ~)

.

CONTRA MUNDUM PRESS

is published by Rainer J. Hanshe
Typography & Design: Alessandro Segalini
Publicity & Marketing: Alexandra Gold
Fundraising & Grant Writing: Madeline Hausmann
Ebook Design: Carlie R. Houser

THE FUTURE OF KULCHUR

THE PROJECT

From major museums like the MoMA to art house cinemas such as Film Forum, cultural organizations do not sustain themselves from sales alone, but from subscriptions, donations, benefactors, and grants.

Since benefactors of Peggy Guggenheim's stature are rare to come by, and receiving large grants from major funding bodies is an infrequent and unreliable source of capital, we seek to further our venture through a form of modest support that is within everyone's reach.

Although esteemed, Contra Mundum is an independent boutique press with modest profit margins. In not having university, state, or institutional backing, other forms of sustenance are required to move us into the future.

Additionally, in the past decade, the reduction of the purchasing budgets across the nation of both public and private libraries has had a severe impact upon publishers, leading to significant decreases in sales, thereby necessitating the creation of alternative means of subsistence.

Because many of our books are translations, our desire for proper remuneration is a persistent point of concern. Even when translators receive grants for book projects, the amount is often insufficient to compensate for their efforts, and royalties, which trickle in slowly over years, are not a reliable source of compensation.

WHAT WILL BE DONE

With your participation we seek to offer writers and translators greater compensation for their work, and in a more expeditious manner.

Additionally, funds will be used to pay for translation rights, basic operating expenses of the press, and to represent our writers and translators at book fairs.

If the means exist, we will also create a translation residency, providing opportunities to both junior and more established translators, thereby furthering our cultural efforts.

Through a greater collective and the cultural commons of the world, we can band together to create this constellation and together function as a patron for the writers and artists published by CMP. We hope you will join us in this partnership.

Your patronage is an expression of your confidence and belief in visionary literary work that would otherwise be exiled from the Anglophone world. With bookstores and presses around the world struggling to survive, and many even closing, joining the Future of Kulchur allows you to be a part of an active force that forms a continuous *&* stable foundation which safeguards the longevity of Contra Mundum Press.

Endowed by your support, we can expand our poetics of hospitality by continuing to publish works from many different languages and reflect, welcome, and embrace the riches of other cultures throughout the world. To become a member of any of our Future of Kulchur tiers is to express your support of such cultural work, and to aid us in continuing it. A unified assemblage of individuals can make a modern Mæcenas and deepen access to radical works.

The Oyster ($2/month)

· Three issues (PDFs) of your choice of our art journal, *Hyperion.*
· 15% discount on all purchases (for orders made directly through our site) during the subscription term (one year).
· Impact: $2 a month contributes to the cost to convert a title to an ebook and make it accessible to wider audiences.

Paris Spleen ($5/month)

- Receive $35 worth of books or your choice from our back catalog.
- Three issues (PDFs) of your choice of our art journal, *Hyperion*.
- 18% discount on all purchases (for orders made directly through our site) during the subscription term (one year).
- Impact: $5 a month contributes to the cost purchasing new fonts for expanding the range of our typesetting palette.

Gilgamesh ($10/month)

- Receive $70 worth books of your choice from our back catalog.
- 4 PDF issues of our magazine *Hyperion*.
- A quarterly newsletter with exclusive content such as interviews with authors or translators, excerpts from upcoming titles, publication news, and more.
- 20% discount on all merchandise (for orders made directly through our site) during the subscription term (one year).
- Select images of our books as they are being typeset.
- Impact: $10 a month contributes to the production and publication of *Hyperion*, encouraging critical engagement with art theory & æsthetics and ensuring we can pay our contributors.

The Greek Music Drama ($25/month)

- Receive $215 worth of books.
- 5 PDF issues of *Hyperion* ($25 value).
- A quarterly newsletter with exclusive content such as interviews with authors or translators, excerpts from upcoming titles, publication news, and more.
- 25% discount (for orders made directly through our site) on all merchandise during the subscription term (one year).
- Impact: $25 a month contributes to the cost of designing and formatting a book.

Citizen Above Suspicion ($50/month)

- Receive $525 worth of books.
- 6 PDF issues of *Hyperion* ($30 value).
- 1 tote.
- A quarterly newsletter with exclusive content such as interviews with authors or translators, excerpts from upcoming titles, publication news, and more.
- 30% discount on all merchandise (for orders made directly through our site) during the subscription term (one year).
- Select one forthcoming book from our catalog and receive it in advance of release to the general public.
- Impact: $50 a month contributes to editorial & proofreading fees.

Casanova ($100/month)

- Receive $1040 worth of books.
- 7 PDF issues of *Hyperion* ($30 value).
- 1 tote.
- A quarterly newsletter with exclusive content such as interviews with authors or translators, excerpts from upcoming titles, publication news, and more.
- 35% discount on all merchandise (for orders made directly through our site) during the subscription term (one year).
- A signed typeset spread from two forthcoming books.
- Select two forthcoming books from our catalog and receive them in advance of release to the general public.
- Impact: $100 a month contributes to the cost of translating a book, therefore supporting a translator in their craft & bringing a new work & perspective to Anglophone audiences.

Cybernetogamic Vampire ($200/month)

- Receive $2020 worth of books.
- 10 PDF issues of *Hyperion* ($50 value).
- 1 tote.
- A quarterly newsletter with exclusive content such as interviews with authors or translators, excerpts from upcoming titles, publication news, and more.
- 40% discount on all merchandise (for orders made directly through our site) during the subscription term (one year).
- A signed typeset spread from four of our forthcoming books.
- The listing of your name in the colophon to a forthcoming book of your choice.
- Select four forthcoming books from our catalog and receive them in advance of release to the general public.
- Impact: $200 a month contributes to general operating expenses of the press, paying for translation rights, and attending book fairs to represent our writers and translators and reach more readers around the world.

To join the Future of Kulchur, visit here:

contramundumpress.com/support-us